IN THE DUKE OF TIME

COPYRIGHT

CHAPTER

ONE

E vie raced into her room that Lady Lupton-Gage was so generous to offer her this Season. Her maid sat on the settee, a small leather valise by her feet and Evie's reticule in her hand.

"Is everything prepared?" she asked, stripping out of her wedding gown before the door had closed. Her maid stood and helped her out of the blue silk and tulle she had worn to celebrate her marriage to Lord Bourbon, but she could not remain with the blaggard.

Not after what she had seen, only two hours after saying, "I do." Evie seethed and fought not to curse at his pitiful excuse of a way to explain his actions. No excuses in the world could make what she had seen forgivable.

Her friends and family would be disappointed she annulled the marriage, but she would not be. Lord Bourbon ought to be glad she had not disclosed his disgraceful actions to the *ton*. To endure a lifetime of his unfaithfulness would not be borne.

"Here, Miss Hall, let me help you into the traveling gown."

Evie stepped into the gray traveling dress, shuffling it over her body and giving her back to Faye so she could button her up. "The carriage should be waiting on Davies Street as you asked," Faye advised.

Evie swallowed her nerves at what her actions would mean. Running away from one's wedding breakfast was scandalous indeed, not to mention she would be shunned from society from this day forward for acting without thought to her reputation.

But then, the image of Lord Bourbon rutting Lady Compton, the widow to the Earl of Compton, in Lord Lupton-Gage's library was a future she could not stomach. How could he? To think she could have had a future with a man who pretended to love her but in truth did not. Was he using her to top up his already significant fortune?

Evie thanked Faye when she handed her a cream spencer. "Lady Lupton-Gage and Arabella will be distracted with the guests for some time, and if we're to leave, we must do so now."

"The staff is presently serving the guests in the ballroom, Miss Hall, so if we slip out the back parlor door and follow the garden path to the side yard and out the gate hidden in the ivy, no one will see. The carriage you hired will be but a few steps down the road. I'm certain of it."

Some of the nerves that Evie suffered calmed at her maid's reassurance. It was imperative they leave London today. She was an heiress, married or not. Lord Lupton-Gage had thankfully ensured she remained in control of her fortune no matter whom she married. No matter the scandal and her ruin, at least she would have financial security. But she could not remain with an unfaithful husband.

How blessed to have had a wealthy, long-lost relative leave her his fortune. A fortune that, with intelligent investment by her London relatives, had grown to an amount that made even her eyes water.

They started downstairs, and true to Faye's word, no other staff was about. "I shall write a letter to my steward, Lord and Lady Lupton-Gage, and Arabella on the road and explain everything." She would seek help from Lord Lupton-Gage in how to secure an annulment. She had not consummated the marriage, therefore, surely, that was enough to be free of him.

"What if Lord Bourbon comes after you, Miss Hall? Will he not grow angry at what you have done?"

The quiver in her maid's voice gave her pause, and she offered Faye a comforting smile. "All will be well," she said. "Once Lord Lupton-Gage knows of what transpired today, what I saw, he will ensure Lord Bourbon is nothing but a bad memory. They may be shocked by my decision, but it is for the best." London had turned out to be a disappointment, and in truth, Evie would be glad to leave it behind. The politics, the false friendships, and the men who refused to give up their mistresses and whores. How could she have been so blind to his deceitful charm?

Laughter carried out into the foyer from the ballroom as they made the last staircase step. Evie quickened her pace, all but running toward the back parlor.

They were almost free of the house. The doors to the gardens beckoned, and with one last look at the spacious, grand home she had come to adore as much as Lord and Lady Lupton-Gage, Evie and her maid slipped into the gardens undetected.

Relief swamped her several minutes later as the hired

carriage she ordered came into view and waited for her on Davies Street.

"Miss Hall," the driver said, tipping his hat.

Faye opened the carriage door, and Evie climbed inside. Faye placed their traveling valises on the floor and joined her. Without waiting for her approval, the carriage lurched forward, and they were on their way.

"And the driver knows we're headed north? That we're to go as far as the horses will carry us before changing the team?"

"Yes, miss. We shall soon be out of London and on our way." Her maid paused, looking out the window, and Evie could see the concern etched on her brow.

Evie reached out and patted Faye's hand. "All will be well. I have enough money to last several weeks, and we're only going to Scotland. I'm certain I should be able to find a small manor house that I can lease and live in quite comfortably. You may agree to stay or return to London. I know Scotland may not be to everyone's taste, but I wish to be away from here. I'm not made for this society. It is too high in the instep, and heiress or not, the nobility look down on me due to my upbringing and past employment."

"I understand, miss. But I think Scotland will be an adventure for you and me. I shall like to stay and assist you if you would let me."

Evie would be lying if she did not admit to the relief coursing through her, knowing she would not be alone. The driver had been paid and agreed to take them as far as Aberdeen, so they would have his protection until then.

All would be well. She had nothing to worry about and soon would be settled in her new home, far, far away from Lord Bourbon and his unfaithful heart.

. . .

4

After changing horses at Hertford and Bedford, the carriage finally rolled to a stop before a posting house in Huntingdon. Evie wiped the tiredness from her eyes and looked out the window. The day was drawing to a close, the dew settling on the ground. They had traveled all day, making good time, but the horses would need to be rested overnight.

Their driver opened the door and tipped his hat. "Miss Hall, we'll need to stay here for the evening. I need to eat and sleep for a time before we can move forward. There will be rooms here to let. I shall stay in the stables. I'll send word to you when I'm ready to continue the journey in the morning if you're willing."

Evie nodded, wanting out of the carriage in any case. How many days would it take for them to travel to Aberdeen? A significant amount of time, she would guess, and already her bottom was feeling far from elated by her decision.

"Thank you, George. I think that is just the thing." Evie alighted into the inn's yard, stretching as best she could before heading indoors to secure a room.

A bath and a good, hearty meal were just what she needed. Once she had completed those necessities only then would she sleep.

She entered the inn and was greeted by the innkeeper and his wife, who welcomed her warmly. "A room, please, a meal and bath if that is not too much trouble."

"Of course, miss..." the innkeeper said. "Would you like a separate room for your maid?"

"Yes, thank you. And my driver will be staying in the stables. Please ensure he is also given a meal."

"Of course. 'Twould be our pleasure," the older lady said with a smile.

It was only a short time before they were ensconced in their rooms, the innkeeper doing all he could to ensure their stay was enjoyable.

Evie walked around the room, taking in the worn furniture that was otherwise clean and well-placed. She glanced out into the inn's yard and watched as the horses that had brought them from London were unhitched and led toward a nearby stall.

A tall, cloaked gentleman trotted into the yard, his arrival pulling the attention of all those within his vicinity. Evie, too, could not stop watching him. His moves were graceful as he dismounted and led his horse to a waiting stable lad who all but bounced with excitement when offered a coin for his troubles.

"Oh, he's a handsome gentleman, miss," Faye murmured at her side, her attention too fixed on the man.

Evie would not disagree, nor would she tell her maid aloud that she thought the same. She may have once been of the same class as Faye, but that was no longer the case. As an heiress already skating on thin ice due to her actions in London, she needed to remain proper and not bring any undue scandal or gossip in her direction.

"Another traveler, heading north or south, I suppose." Just then, a light knock sounded on the door, and several maids started delivering buckets of steaming-hot water.

"I shall bathe and then rest," she informed Faye. "Due to the length of travel we have before us, you are more than welcome to do the same. You do not need to remain here on my account. I know you too must be exhausted."

"Oh, thank you, Miss Hall. I would like to sleep if you're sure," Faye said.

Evie escorted Faye out of the room before shutting and locking her door, finally enabling them finally to rest for the remainder of the night.

CHAPTER

TWO

E vie woke with a start and stared as a dark figure huddled over the fire in her room, kicking at the logs before stumbling backward.

Fear curled in her stomach, and she reached for the candlestick beside her bed, the cold metal stealing a shiver down her spine.

"Get out," she yelled, holding the blankets up to her chest. Her breath rapidly rose and fell, and she felt her eyes widen when the figure stumbled toward her, peering through the dark as if she were the uninvited intruder.

"Get out?" he stated, his brogue slurred and with a thick Scottish accent. "How about you get out? This is my room, and I paid for it for the night. Best that you get that pretty little face of yours out instead."

Forgetting her modesty and prickled by his arrogance, she kneeled on the bed, glaring at the man. Watching him, she realized where she had seen him before. He was the cloaked gentleman from the inn yard who had arrived earlier this evening.

So he was also staying at the inn? "Well, I'm sorry to tell

you, sir, but you're in my room, so perhaps you ought to go back into the passageway and find the correct room you paid for because this is not it."

When he chuckled, Evie crossed her arms and ground her teeth. The nerve of the man.

"A fiery lass, hey." He stumbled over to the bed, towering above her like some mythical god, and with the fire illuminating him from behind, she wasn't certain that he was not. "And a pretty one, too. What are you doing all alone at this inn? Do you know it's not safe in these parts?"

"I'm not alone. I have a maid and a driver, who are sleeping nearby." She raised her chin, not appreciating that the sight of his chiseled jaw, shadowed by a day's growth of stubble, made him look unfashionably good-looking. Not to mention, when he grinned, his teeth looked white and healthy.

Not an impoverished person then, not that she thought so the moment she had seen him in the yard outside. No person of limited means rode a horse of its breeding or wore a cloak made of such high-quality cloth.

He chuckled and swayed, and she feared he might topple onto the bed. "Come now, lass. I know your type. Tell me, how much will it cost me to bed you? If you require a good tumble and coin, I'm happy to oblige, but you could have just asked me in the tavern. No need to sneak into my room to gain what you want."

Evie felt her mouth gape, and she reached for the blankets and covered herself when his salacious interest slid over her body like a caress. Would he continue this absurdity? Why would he not understand what she was saying?

Possibly because he was too foxed for clear thought...

"Listen here, sir. I'm not a whore, and this is my room, so unless you wish for me to scream until my lungs burn and your ears ring, I suggest you depart this room and forget that you ever accosted me so abruptly in the middle of the night."

Something in her tone or words seemed to give him pause, and he frowned, taking in the room more than he had up until then. His gaze settled on her valise and her traveling gown that lay over a chair, ready for tomorrow's journey.

He stepped back from the bed, running a hand through his hair. "Now that you mention it, the bed is...the bed is situated on the wrong wall. How odd. I could have sworn it was on the other side of the room when I checked in this afternoon."

Evie pursed her lips and stared at him, nonplussed. The man was an oaf and a fool and was making himself look even the bigger one every moment he debated her words.

"You see, this is not your room, sir. Please leave," she stated, pointing toward the door. "And do not come back."

He turned on his heel, stumbled, and fell face-first against the floor. A horrible sound accompanied his fall, and without thinking, Evie went to him, assisting him in sitting up as best she could.

He had scuffed his forehead, and already a trickle of blood ran down his brow. Evie reached for the small, clean handkerchief beside her bed and held it against his wound. "There must have been a small tack or rock on the floor when you fell. I'm sorry to say, but you're bleeding."

"I am?" he asked, reaching up and placing his hand atop hers.

Evie fought the nerves that fluttered in her stomach at his touch. He had large, calloused hands that covered hers as if she were not a full-grown woman. Strength radiated from him, and had he wished, there would have been no possible way she could have fought off his advances.

But he had not. He was leaving up until the point he tripped, and the fear she had but moments ago vanished.

"All will be well. I think it is just a scratch." She kneeled before him, holding pressure to his wound. She cupped his cheek, keeping him still, and could sense his gaze on her.

"As foxed as I am, and if this is indeed your room, I do apologize, but I will not be sorry for drinking in your beauty. You are quite the sight for my tired eyes."

Evie swallowed and fought not to blush at his words. Not that he would see her rosy cheeks, not in the dimly lit room mainly illuminated by the fire.

"Well, for a drunkard, you're not so bad. I'm certain there are worse fellows in the world who could have stumbled into my room."

He chuckled. "It would be wise to lock your door upon my departure. There are several men downstairs of questionable manners, and I would hate to have to shoot one of them dead should they attempt anything with you. I have much to do and a long way to travel yet, and dealing with such unlawful actions would delay my journey a day or so."

Evie grinned and met his eyes. Even in the shadows, she could see they burned with an emotion she could not place. Or at least one she did not want to. It was scandalous enough that he was still in her room. Should anyone come in and see her kneeling before him, cupping his cheek as if to kiss his very alluring lips, she would be ruined.

Her gaze dipped to his lips at her thought, and warmth settled between her thighs. She was a scandalous minx. How could she find him so tempting, so compelling?

"You ought to stop looking at me as if you wish to eat

me alive, miss. It does not help my roguish self who wants to misbehave."

Evie bit her lip. She should heed his warning. He was a stranger, a man she would never see again, more the pity, and still she tempted fate, poked the lion that growled before her without any barriers separating them.

"I'm not looking at you any differently than anyone else in the world. You may have hit your head harder than you think."

"Really," he said, his voice low and alluring. His hand settled on her knee, and goosebumps skittled across her skin. "So you do not feel anything for me? I do not tempt you at all?"

"Of course not," she said, but even she could hear the tremble in her voice, the longing, the need that would not keep quiet and still in the back of her mind.

"Well then," he said, hoisting himself to stand. The handkerchief stuck to his head, and Evie fought not to laugh. "I bid you goodnight," he said, bowing and leaving her on the floor as if they had not almost kissed.

Well, she thought they may have almost kissed, but then, she had never been kissed before, so maybe she was incorrect in her estimation.

As he suggested, she stood and went to the door, throwing the bolt across and, for good measure, pushed a small bedside cupboard in front of it for extra security.

She would hate to tempt fate a second time, not entirely confident that if that particular gentleman stumbled into her room again, she would be so keen to remove him.

THREE

After breaking her fast in her bedroom the following morning, it wasn't long before they were back on the road, traveling north and gaining miles between London and all that Evie had left behind.

Although she was uncertain if she would ever return south, her plans for the future were set. She would lease a small manor house in a quiet village near the sea and enjoy her independence away from the glittering *ton* who, no matter how much she tried, would never accept her.

Her maid snored and startled herself in sleep before slumping back against the window. Evie pulled out a book she had slipped into her valise and used its hardcover to attempt a letter to Arabella.

She would first apologize and beg for forgiveness for leaving her in town. Arabella, having come from a similar background to hers, had found society cutting and difficult to maneuver. But should her actions in leaving her husband sink her reputation forever, she had not wanted to take Arabella down with her. That would not have been fair at all. Next she would write to Lord and Lady Lupton-Gage and explain a second time.

A gunshot rang out, and one of the windows in the carriage burst into a million pieces. Glass shattered into the interior, and Evie stilled, shocked by what had occurred, before self-preservation kicked in. She grabbed hold of Faye, not as wide awake as she was, and pulled her onto the floor.

Their carriage driver shouted something Evie could not make out before the carriage lurched forward in speed. Were they trying to outrun some shooting madman?

"Is it a highwayman? We're done for," Faye screamed, tears filling her eyes.

Evie could not believe it would be so. Surely, they would not be so unlucky.

Her money...

She reached into her pocket and pulled the few notes she had brought with her free. Looking about the carriage, she searched for a place to stash it so it would not be stolen.

The corner of the seat was ripped, and she stuffed it within as quickly as her fingers would work while also trying not to increase the size of the rip and cause it to be obvious she had hidden her funds.

She placed fifty pounds into her pocket, hoping that would be enough to satisfy the highwaymen from searching for more if they were caught.

"We're going to be shot. What if they assault us, Miss Hall?"

Evie pulled Faye into her arms and shushed her concerns. "All will be well. Just do not mention I'm an heiress or that I'm carrying funds. I have kept enough blunt on me to please them, hopefully."

Faye's eyes flew wide, her face pale. "Of course, I will not say a word."

Several more gunshots rang out, and Faye sobbed. Evie leaned over her, protecting her maid as best she could. A cold shiver ran through her blood when their driver shouted in pain, and the carriage started to slow.

Had they shot George? Was he dying at this very moment?

Fighting back her panic, she dared not move once the carriage rolled to a stop. Men's voices sounded outside, along with laughter. Evie prayed they would not be injured and would come away from today maybe a little lighter on blunt, but nothing else.

Please do not hurt us...

The carriage door wrenched open, and Evie came face-to-face with a man, a bandana covering his dirty, dusty face. His hair was unwashed and unkempt, and the stench that filled the carriage from his person made her eyes water.

"Out with ye, pretty ladies. Let us see what we have here."

Evie did as he said, helping Faye to join her. Her maid sobbed, unable to control the fear that plagued her every move.

"Shut ye friend up, or I'll shut her up. Can't stand a babbling woman."

Evie pulled Faye a little behind her. "All will be well, Faye. Please try to do as he says." Her maid, thankfully, stopped crying, but Evie could feel the tension echoing from her body, her fingers clutched tight around hers.

"I can see ye maid has no valuables, but what about you, love?" Another man pulled her valise out of the vehicle and rummaged through it, her carefully packed clothing strewn over the dusty ground.

"I have money, sir, but you will only find clothes in my bag. We're traveling north for work."

The greedy man's eyes lit with interest at her mention of funds. "Where is this money you speak of? Here?" he asked, stepping close and pulling the bodice of her gown out, looking down at her breasts.

Heat kissed every part of her body as revulsion shivered down her spine. The highwayman licked his lips as if the thought of tasting her floated through his mind before his hand slid down her side, scandalously close to the under-side of her breast.

Evie swallowed a scream, something telling her to remain calm and not react. The man was a predator, and if she ran, she could not help but think he would chase and the games would be afoot.

"Is it in your gown somewhere?" he asked, his hand against her hip. He found the pocket and reached inside. Evie gasped when he reached farther and touched her cunny.

Tears prickled her eyes, but she dared not move, not slap him, not do anything. Frozen in fear, his eyes crinkled with a smile beneath his bandana, and she knew he was enjoying himself.

"Ah, here it is." He clasped the money in her pocket and pulled it out, the surprise crossing his face at the fifty-pound note.

"For hired help, you carry a lot of blunt." He held up his horde and waved it before the other men, all wearing bandanas, and as filthy as their leader.

"I have been saving for several years," she lied. "That is all that I have in the world."

The bandit threw back his head and laughed. "Ahh, well, now it is mine. I thank ye for your hard work and will bid ye good day."

Evie dared only move once the men were atop their horses, galloping away into the forest surrounding them. Only then did she move toward the front of the carriage, where their driver had remained unnervingly quiet during the ordeal.

The young man was slumped over the seat, and blood oozed from his arm and covered the side of his clothing.

"Help me, Faye. George's been shot." She climbed up to the driver's seat and inspected his arm. Needing to stem the flow, she looked around for what she could use and noticed George wore a cravat. Untying it, she slipped it around his arm and fastened it, glad to see the blood stopped oozing at such a profound rate.

Faye joined her and helped sit George up, but how to move him? How to get them away from here and to the next village?

The sound of a cantering horse pulled her attention to the road, and she waved down a single rider coming in their direction of travel. "Sir! Sir! Please help us." Evie watched, something about the man pulling at a memory before she remembered where she had seen him. In her room, cradled in her arms as his brow bled.

Dear Lord in Heaven, anyone but him...

"What has happened here?" he asked, his Scottish accent thick with every word he spoke and yet not slurred this morning from too much wine.

"Highwaymen pulled us over, and our driver has been shot."

The horseman looked about the carriage and, seeing her clothes and all the possessions she had strewn about the road, jumped down from his horse, tying it to the carriage.

He climbed up and joined them, and only then did she see the moment he recognized her. A muscle worked in his jaw before he turned his attention to George, feeling her driver's neck. Did he think he was dead? Had George died, and she had not noticed?

"He's alive but needs a doctor. There is one at the next village, a good three miles away, but he will make it if we travel in haste.

"Can we place him in the carriage? How will we get him down?"

Without a by your leave, the Scotsman bent and picked up George, placing him over his shoulder and climbing back down, depositing him on the carriage floor as if he weighed nothing but a feather.

For several heartbeats, Evie stared, unable to comprehend how a man could do such a thing, be so strong, and not even break into a sweat.

Perhaps he was a god, after all.

"I've tied my horse to the back of the carriage, and I shall drive you all to the next village. Pack up your belongings, and let us go."

Evie helped Faye down, and with the aid of her maid, they shoved her clothes back in her valise and climbed into the carriage.

"Hold on. I shall push the horses to ensure we put enough distance between us and the highwaymen."

Evie glanced at Faye and did as he suggested. Their driver groaned on the floor, and Evie prayed he would live. But what would they do if he did not? What were they to do without him? She could not return to London. That was not an option. She had not thought highwaymen would rob them.

Could this week become any more of a catastrophe? She did not think so at this very moment.

FOUR

B y the time they arrived at the next village of Huntingdon, George was poorly indeed. He had continued to slip in and out of consciousness, and for several moments before the town came into sight, Evie was sure that he had died.

The carriage traveled at a breakneck speed that would have typically terrified her, but something about the man driving them gave her cause to keep her fears at bay.

Thankfully, after what felt like an eternity, the carriage rolled to a stop before a small, quaint cottage with roses growing up the front of the building, and even from where she sat, she could smell the sweet scent of the flowers.

Having seen their hasty arrival, an older gentleman walked out into the picketed front garden and gave a friendly wave. "What can I do you for?" Evie heard him ask. The carriage lurched to one side as their driver jumped down, going to speak to the man who, with any luck, was the village doctor.

"I came across this carriage. Highwaymen have shot the

driver in the arm, I believe. Can you help him?" he asked, his Scottish brogue deep and commanding.

"Of course, let me help you carry him inside."

Evie stepped down from the carriage and helped Faye, who had not stopped fidgeting from the moment George had been shot. They moved out of the way to allow the doctor and Scotsman access to George. He groaned at being repositioned but said little else, before being carried indoors.

Evie waited outside, not wanting to get in the way. Faye paced the front gardens, biting her nails, her eyes welling with tears.

"I'm certain George will be well, Faye. There is no reason to panic just yet."

Her maid looked at her so wretchedly that Evie did not know what to say or do. "Are you acquainted with George? I promise we shall do all we can to get him better and back on his feet."

"Oh, Miss Hall, I'm so sorry I did not say before, but George is my sweetheart. We're hoping to marry when we've saved a little money. I wanted to tell you, but I did not want to burden you further with everything happening in London."

Evie stared at Faye for several heartbeats, uncertain how she should react to such news. "So you're stepping out with George? Does this mean you'll wish to stay here while he recuperates?"

Evie felt the world around her spin at the thought of traveling farther north alone. What if more heathens wished to rob her? Who would accompany her and give her respectability?

Faye worked her hands at her front. "If you would allow, Miss Hall. I'm so sorry to do this to you, but I love

George dearly, and I could not face leaving him behind, not knowing if he would survive."

Evie sighed, longing ripping through her that she had never felt such feelings for another. She had not even had the chance to allow her mediocre affections toward her husband to grow after seeing him do what he had.

"I understand, I do, and of course, if you wish to stay, you must. I would not force you to do anything that would cause you or George pain." She clasped Faye's hand and led her toward the house. "Come, we shall see how the doctor is faring with him now."

"I promise, Miss Hall, we'll join you in Aberdeen when George is well enough. Please keep our positions open. Traveling to another country has always been a dream for us, and we do not want what has happened today to hinder our plans to work for you and see a little more of the world."

"Of course," Evie agreed, liking that she would see Faye and George again. Faye had greatly supported her these past weeks, especially after seeing what Lord Bourbon had done to her on their wedding day. She could not say no to Faye now. Not in her time of need.

"I will not replace either of you, and I look forward to your arrival."

After leaving Faye with her beloved, Evie had driven the carriage to the nearby inn, fetched her valise, collected her hidden money from the seat, then took a room. She had not seen the Scotsman, having no idea where he had ventured. Upon leaving the doctor's house, she had noted his horse was unhitched from the carriage, and he was nowhere to be seen.

Maybe he, too, had continued his journey north. She had gifted Faye more than enough funds to keep her and George while he healed and said she would send word to the doctor of her address in Scotland when settled.

All that was left to do now was find a new driver to Scotland and be on her way as soon as may be. A more straightforward thought said than done. With nothing left to do, Evie made her way to the taproom, searching for the innkeeper.

He stood behind the bar, a soiled apron covering his worn white shirt and a disgruntled look on his face after having stern words with a rowdy patron.

"What can I do for ye, love?" he asked.

He was a tall gentleman and as round as he was high, but he had kind eyes and gave her hope for some assistance. "My carriage driver was injured earlier today, but I need to travel on to Scotland. Do you know of anyone who would drive me north? I can pay them handsomely for their time and trouble. I will also require a maid."

The innkeeper stroked his jaw and long beard, thinking over her request. "I cannot think of anyone to be ye maid, miss, but I shall inquire regarding a driver if you wish?"

"Thank you, that is most kind of you," she said, disappointed by his words, hoping she could have traveled a little farther north today. "If there is no one to help me, can you please ensure my carriage is ready to depart tomorrow morning at first light? I shall drive myself if I cannot hire a person to do so." She ignored his surprise at her words and stepped away before she remembered her second request. "Oh, and I require a gun. If you would be so kind as to find one of those for me as well, thank you."

The innkeeper grinned but agreed before Evie left for her room.

Unfortunately, by the morning and after a restless night from the bar below being rowdier than expected, she walked out into the inn's yard and stared at her carriage, hitched with two brown mares and no driver up on his post waiting for her.

She sighed and placed her bag under the carriage seat before climbing onto the box. The carriage seemed higher than yesterday, and her stomach fluttered, hoping she did not get lost or fall off. Evie took stock of her surroundings and noted the pair of flintlocks on her seat. She placed them in her bag and picked up the reins.

She had driven a carriage before, of course, but they had all been short trips. Today would be several miles. But how hard could it be? Men did this every day and did not struggle. Surely, she could not get into any more trouble than had already befallen her.

And she needed to keep moving. If Lord Bourbon was following close on her heels, she wanted to be as far from England as soon as possible.

The horses, a well-trained pair, did as she instructed, and she was soon walking them out of the inn yard and onto the village's main thoroughfare. Not that the small hamlet was busy at this time of the morning, and no one seemed to care that a woman was driving a carriage alone.

Evie made her way onto the north road and prayed everything would work out. She had two guns, loaded and ready if needed, and if the worst happened to her, she would merely throw all her money at any future bandits and pray they would leave her alone for good this time.

She could always replace her money, but not her life.

After an hour of traveling north, the boredom of being

alone, of watching two horses' rumps trot before her, and the cooling breeze that grew colder with each step they took started to wane.

She had forgotten to ask the innkeeper how far away the next village would be and how many hours that would take via carriage. Not to mention, after several miles, she had not seen another rider or carriage, and fear crept up her spine that she had taken a wrong turn or had continued north on some road that was not the one she was supposed to be on.

What if she were lost? What if the town never came into sight before nightfall?

She swallowed her fears and pressed on, started to hum a tune that her mama used to sing to her when she was scared as a child. Relief and trepidation filled her at the cloaked figure who sat atop a sizable horse on the side of the road.

Was he another highwayman? Did he mean her harm? She reached for her valise and pulled out a flintlock, settling it on her lap. Evie did not slow her carriage, not wanting to let the man know that she was intimidated by his appearance.

But upon approaching, she recognized the gentleman as the one who had assisted them the day before, except his features were far less pleasing or welcoming, for that matter.

In fact, he looked downright murderous, even more so than the highwaymen who had shot George.

She schooled her features and tipped her head in greeting as she trotted past before he pushed his mount beside her horses, clasping their reins and pulling her carriage to a halt.

"What the hell are you doing, woman?" he yelled, his brogue thick in anger.

"Driving to Scotland. What are you doing touching my horse's reins?" she argued back, unwilling to let him think he could bully her in such a way. She was not a child, nor did she need his permission to be on this road.

"Are you trying to get yourself killed? You need to turn back, return to your home, and stop this madness that almost got you and your servants killed yesterday."

Evie raised her chin, narrowing her eyes. "Really, and are you going to make me?" she challenged.

His eyes narrowed also. "If I must."

CHAPTER
FIVE

arvey fought to keep his temper in check. The
woman was clearly addled of the mind and
perhaps still traumatized from her run-in with
the highwaymen the day before.

Even so, she had to see sense. Traveling alone, driving a carriage on this secluded north road, was not a wise choice for the woman. She would end up either dead or have unthinkable things occur to her that could make her wish for the former.

"You have several more miles to drive before reaching the next town, and you cannot possibly think you're capable of keeping this team in check and remaining alert enough to drive them for that period of time."

She set her mouth into a determined line, and he took in her features for the first time since meeting her yesterday.

She was a pretty woman, her cheeks rosy from the cool air and being outdoors. Her hair had become loose from her coiffure, and several golden strands lay against her shoulders.

His attention dipped lower still, and he could not deny that he liked what he saw, even if the woman was being a pain in his ass and needed to turn about and grow some sense.

"I have managed this far without any trouble and have two flintlocks. I'm more than capable of keeping myself safe, Mister..." she hedged, seeking his name.

He would not give her one. Not yet, not until he had gained her agreement and left this absurd plan of hers. "And what are you to do when you arrive in Scotland? Have you thought of that?" he asked, not caring if she understood his brogue that grew thicker with the increasing aggravation she raised within him.

"I'm going to lease a house or small cottage. Not that I need to explain anything to you, mister whatever your name is and who wishes to remain anonymous." She crossed her arms, forgetting that she held reins, and soon dropped them back into her lap.

"You will find such plans hard to achieve. Most cottages are leased to the tenant farmers, and I can tell you now that a laird or land owner will not toss out their people for a Sassenach."

Her mouth opened with a gasp before snapping closed. "Well, I do not care what you think of my wishes. I shall do as I please and will do it with or without your help."

"Do use that brain within your pretty head, lass, and do as I say before it is too late." Harvey turned his mount away from the carriage and cantered ahead, moving into the trees and out of sight. He would, of course, watch the carriage from afar, keep her safe until the next village if she did not turn about and go home as she should.

Not that he would tell the little hellion of his care, but some parts of the roads about England and Scotland were not for the faint of heart and certainly not for the fairer sex.

He just hoped he did not need to save her from herself.

———

After many hours, too many to count, Evie pulled the carriage up before The Rose Inn in Lincoln and threw the reins to the waiting stableman.

She climbed down, her legs as tired as her eyes, her hands stinging from holding the reins for so many hours.

Before continuing, she would purchase gloves and hope they would help protect her already-injured palms.

The innkeeper welcomed her as she made her way indoors. The thought of a hot meal, bath, and bed beckoned her like nothing else ever in her life.

Well, except maybe telling the too-high-in-the-instep man on the road who tried to warn her away from her goals. Her sanctuary away from London and Lord Bourbon.

"While we're preparing you a room, miss, would you like to dine in our private parlor? There is another gentleman in there at present, but a maid is always present, so it is quite proper, I assure you." The innkeeper turned and glanced into the rowdy taproom. "A better option for a lady like yourself than in there," he said, tipping his head toward the taproom door.

"I would welcome that, thank you." The innkeeper led her into a rectangular dining room with several round tables. A large fire burned in the grate, and the square-panelled window overlooked the village's main street.

Evie's steps faltered before the gentleman diner. The very one who had cantered off into the afternoon only hours before, leaving her alone on the road.

Not that she expected him to keep her safe or drive her to the next village, but he could have kept her company. Rode alongside her vehicle and spoke of his country or some such. He was a Scotsman after all. Surely, he knew more of the northern land she traveled to than she did.

He glanced up, and his slow blink of annoyance sparked another bout of fury within her. Schooling her features and refusing to give way to an act of a banshee that the Scots people often thought existed, she sat at a table the furthermost from him and settled her dusty skirts.

"We have stew this evening, miss. Would you like a plate and a glass of our best wine?" the innkeeper asked, trying his best to be hospitable.

"That sounds delicious, thank you." Evie sat silently for several minutes, watching the Scotsman ignore her presence and eat his meal with maddening slowness. Not that she downed her meals with speed, not anymore at least, but there had been a time when eating occurred during the times the above stairs ate, and so hastiness was in order so as not to miss out.

"More wine, thank you," she heard him ask the maid waiting to serve them both in the room.

Another glass was promptly poured, and Evie could no longer hold back her annoyance. "Did you have an enjoyable solitary ride this afternoon, sir? Mine," she said, continuing as if she did not care to hear his answer, "was long and arduous. If only I had company for the many hours I had to travel alone. At least then, it would have broken up the monotonous lulling that the horses create when one is seated behind them with very little to do but to look between their ears."

He sighed and leaned back in his chair. The slow turn of his head to look at her oozed with mockery. "I did tell you to return south. Your journey back to the village where you left your servants would have been much shorter than the one you are in now. It is not my fault that you do not listen."

Evie bit her tongue, fighting the urge to rail at him for being right, but also so uppity about the whole thing. Did he have to boast so much?

She pushed her chair back and went to his table, sitting beside him.

His brows rose, but he did not tell her to move. A good sign perhaps? "While I know it is odd to see a woman traveling alone to Scotland, the Highlands in particular, I do have my reasons. And up until yesterday, I did have a chaperone and driver, who will join me once George is well enough to do so. They're sweethearts, you see, and I could not separate them, no matter how much I would have liked company on my journey north."

At her rambling, he stared at her as if she were the most boring woman on the planet. Evie stared back at him, arrested by his deep green eyes and long lashes.

Gosh, up close this Scotsman was more handsome than she first thought. A little flutter of nerves settled in her stomach, and she pushed them away. She did not need to lose concentration because the man before her had a handsome visage.

"In any case, I require a driver, and you seem to be heading north yourself, so I'm throwing myself at your mercy and begging you to escort me. I will pay handsomely, however much you want, but please help me and know that I shall do this with or without your help, but I would prefer not to do it unaided."

Again, he stared at her for several minutes before picking up his napkin and wiping his face. "How much are you willing to pay me for my troubles? And after meeting you and our interactions this day, I'm certain that my troubles when it comes to you will be great indeed."

Evie bit back a grin and fought not to woot with glee. Was he going to agree? Did she have a chance to travel with a Scotsman to Scotland and not be so vulnerable?

"Ten pounds?"

His face did not change at her sum, and she debated if she had stated too much or not enough.

"Make it twenty, and I'm all yours, lass."

Evie did smile then and held out her hand, wishing to shake on their bargain. "It's a deal then?" she asked.

His hand, large, calloused, and strong, engulfed hers, and she shivered anew. "It's a deal, lass."

CHAPTER

SIX

The following day, as promised, her new Scottish driver waited for her in the inn yard, standing beside his horse, which he had tied to the back of her carriage.

Evie surveyed him for several moments, his cooing, deep voice as he spoke to his horse making her curious as to what he would sound like when seducing a woman.

There was something about the man that drew the eyes and not only hers if the few maids who worked at the inn and ogled him near the kitchen doors were any indication.

So tall and handsome, broad-shouldered and strong.

"Mister," she said, coming up behind him and tapping him on the shoulder. He twisted about and stared down at her as if she were an annoying field mouse.

"Can I help you further?" he asked, his tone mocking.

"You have not introduced yourself to me. I'm Miss Evie Hall. Originally from Brighton but recently London. And you?" she asked, falling into his deep green eyes that watched her like a hawk.

"Your Grace, a basket from the kitchen. Until we see you again, have a pleasant journey north."

The innkeeper handed over a large basket, supposedly full of food and wine, for the duke and their journey north...

A duke!

"You're a duke?" she all but squeaked, dipping into a curtsy, certain that was what she was supposed to do when around such nobility.

The innkeeper frowned at her exclamation as if she had lost her mind, which after finding out such a truth, maybe she had.

He tipped his head, his mouth pulled into an annoyed line. "I'm Harvey James, Duke of Ruthven, Laird of Cheyne when in Scotland. You may call me Your Grace in England and my lord in Scotland." He placed the basket inside the carriage and set down the stairs.

Without asking, he took her hand and led her into the carriage, slamming the door closed before she could utter another word. Not that she could think of forming more. He was a laird too!

She had wanted to escape London and all the nobility who were fibbers and cheats, and somehow, she had hired the very kind of person she had been trying to avoid.

Not that she thought him a liar and a cheat, but he was still nobility, part of their fickle little club that she would never be welcome into. Not really, no matter how wealthy she may be.

She lowered the carriage window to speak to him. "If you do not wish to escort me, Your Grace, I understand. I know your time is valuable, and escorting a woman you know nothing about was not on your list to do when returning to Scotland."

He sighed, meeting her gaze. "Granted, escorting you

north was not in my plans, but you're compensating me, and I'm happy to do so. I'm traveling to Aberdeenshire, where to were you looking to end your journey?"

Evie bit her lip, unsure how he would react to the news that Aberdeen was where she wanted to go. Would he think she was following him? How mortifying if he did.

"Aberdeenshire will work for me, and you do not have to answer now, but if you have a spare cottage or know of one available in a village in this locale, mayhap you could help me gain a lease on one. I don't ever intend to return to London."

"You now wish for my service in finding a house for you?" He crossed his arms. "And how do you intend to pay for all your plans, Miss Hall?"

Evie would not tell him she could pay for many things as the heiress she was, but a little of the truth would not hurt. "I worked hard and saved," she lied, knowing her pitiful wage as a maid would never have gone far enough to save even a shilling. She was just fortunate enough to inherit her fortune, which she would not squander. "I can lease a cottage or small manor house. I merely need help finding accommodations, and with the assistance of a laird, my chances of not being cheated greatly improve. Please help me, Your Grace," she asked, reverting to begging if need be.

Harvey clamped his jaw shut, ignoring her pouty lips and beckoning eyes as she asked him for assistance. How could he refuse a woman in need? He could not, even if helping her would mean spending more time in her company, which grew more difficult by the hour.

He'd never seen such an unassuming beauty in his life.

Most women threw themselves at his head, and pretty runaways from London, he had no doubt, would do the same. He narrowed his eyes, wondering what her story was. She had a maid and driver, not entirely without means then, but was she nobility, gentry, or merely a wealthy tradesman's daughter?

He supposed he could be accommodating this once. They were traveling to the same locale, after all.

"Very well. I shall see what housing is available in the village near my estate. Now, close the window and settle back in the squabs. We'll travel for several hours until lunch and break our fast along the road."

"There is no village between here and our next stop?" she asked.

"There is, but we need no more distractions or extended breaks, so we will rest the horses but keep on the road."

Harvey climbed onto the box and picked up the reins, clicking his tongue and urging the horses forward. They drove for several hours until the sun was high in the sky, even if clouds marred its glow sporadically throughout the day, deluging him in the occasional shower.

He found a nearby stream and unhitched the horses. After watering them, he tied them to a nearby tree to rest. Miss Hall set out the picnic, which the innkeeper's wife had packed for them, and pulled out a carriage blanket to lay on the damp grass to sit.

The next time he traveled through Lincoln, he would be sure to thank the innkeeper's wife for her kindness and reimburse them for their trouble.

He joined Miss Hall, seating himself with the picnic basket between them, and tried to ignore that their little journey north, without a chaperone, was against all the rules of a gentleman. To anyone, they appeared as if they were runaway lovers, unmarried and scandalous. He would never find a wealthy bride to save his estates if he was marred with such tainted history.

"Traveling together and alone, I think it would be best that we pretend to be husband and wife," he blurted without thinking. "Most people know me over the border, but we can stay at inns I do not frequent and travel under an alias. I think this would be best. Your reputation would not be sullied, and questions would not be asked if I'm your spouse."

Miss Hall, who had been sipping the wine with great relish, choked on her beverage at his words. He remained quiet as she fought to regain her composure. "Married? But, will the innkeepers think we should stay in the same room when we stop for the evenings? I cannot do that, Your Grace," she said, her face paling.

"It is common for husbands and wives to sleep in different rooms. My parents, before they passed, never occupied the same bed, and it will not look odd if we do the same. But we cannot continue in this way. People will talk, and before you even reach Aberdeen, you will be known as a fallen woman, fast, unless..." he paused, meeting her gaze. "There is truth in my words?" he asked.

"I'm not a whore if that is what you're asking me, Your Grace. I may not be nobility like you, but I'm not a fallen woman either. I'm just a woman who wishes for a life of my own, far from London. There is no crime in that."

Her words made his lips twitch, and he could under-stand her sentiment and the censure in her tone at his questioning. "I'm delighted to hear it. I would not want to be part of anything untoward. I am a duke, after all, and society, whether you like it or not, holds me to a standard I'm loath to tumble from." She watched him and did not respond, but he wanted to know more, everything if she would tell him. "Will you not disclose why you're running away from London? Were you unhappy there? Were you mistreated?" Harvey could not think such a thing possible, but odder things had occurred so he could not discount it.

"London did not suit," she said, biting her lip in thought. "I was not cut from the same cloth as you, Your Grace, and as a woman of independent means, as humble as those means are against yours, nothing I did would ever be enough no matter what level of society I hailed from." She quieted a moment, and he could see she chose her words carefully. "I did not like where my life headed and knew that if I did not leave, I would end up miserable. Therefore, I chose a different path for myself, and I shall see it through to the end if you will help me."

She wished for a happy life.

He could understand her wanting a fresh start, a new life. He, too, had done similarly, taking control of the finances his father had run into the ground, turning the estates around so they may be once again profitable. Enough so that he could marry well. An heiress would also aid his financial woes.

"Well," he said, picking up the bottle of wine and taking a healthy sip. "To your future happiness. Shall you gain all that you wish for."

She smiled, and her pretty features took his breath away. He downed another sip, ignoring the fire that ignited in his soul at her joy.

"To our future happiness. Are we not husband and wife now?" she teased, her grin pulling one from him also.

"Of course, to us," he repeated, not entirely disliking how that sounded.

SEVEN

T he carriage rolled into Doncaster just after dusk. The village houses had their curtains drawn and candles burning by the time Harvey pulled the carriage to a stop. The innkeeper greeted them, taking their bags and ensuring he would prepare their separate rooms posthaste.

Harvey stretched as he waited for Miss Hall to join him. She stepped down from the carriage and looked with interest about the yard before her direct and confident gaze collided with his.

"Can you hear that?" she asked, walking over to him, a slight frown between her perfectly arched brows.

Harvey listened carefully, and floating on the darkening night air was the whisper of music and, every so often, the murmurings of laughter and conversation.

"You, boy," Harvey asked the stable lad, unhitching their horses. "What is that celebration we can hear?" he asked.

The young lad smiled and pointed down the street. "That's the yearly village dance, sir. You're more than welcome to attend," the young lad said, unaware of his status or how he should be addressed. He'd never stayed in Doncaster before, having usually passed through it to stay at Ferrybridge, which he preferred when traveling north or south.

"Do you mean there is a ball?" Miss Hall clasped his arm and jumped up and down at his side. "May we go, husband? I so wish to dance," she cooed.

He narrowed his eyes, not expecting her to use their ploy so publicly and quickly since they had just spoken of it earlier this afternoon.

"Are you not tired, my love?" he asked. "Do you not wish to rest instead?"

She pouted, and the stable hand chuckled, mumbling under his breath something oddly like he had little chance of sleeping.

"I'm not tired at all, and a dance will be just the thing to ensure a good night's rest."

That was probably partially true, but Harvey could think of other things they could do that would lead to a restful sleep. He stopped that thought and threw it aside. He was not, in truth, married to the woman at his side. Bedding her, as enjoyable as he believed that may be, was not an entanglement he needed to get himself wrapped up in.

With nothing else to do and not ready for bed just yet, Harvey held out his arm and decided to indulge Miss Hall in her wish. She took his arm, smiling at him as if he were her whole world, a notion as far from the truth as they were husband and wife.

He started toward where the boy had pointed, and within a minute or so, the town hall came into view, the music growing louder with each step.

"We're not dressed for a dance. Do you suppose the people will mind?" Miss Hall asked him.

He shook his head, doubting the people would be as judgemental as society back in London. "I think we shall blend in perfectly fine. Do not think another moment on our attire."

The hall was bursting at the seams with people. The rectangular-shaped building had sconces on the walls, and several hanging candelabras lit the room, leaving no shadow to hide.

Even though a small village—the people and the room, with its flowers and colorful gowns, the men and ladies both in their best—it made Harvey think he was stepping into Almack's for the second time.

Once was enough for Almack's, but the laughter, dancing, and sight of people enjoying each other's company without the politics and games that Society often played was refreshing.

"Will you do me the honor?" he asked Miss Hall.

She giggled, and he could not hold back the twist of his lips. "I would love to dance, husband."

He led her onto the floor. No locals gaped or spoke of them, gossiping as to who they were. They made room for them both and allowed them to join the celebrations.

Not long after they had taken a step of the minuet, the dance ended, and the first notes of a waltz began to play.

Miss Hall stared at him with eyes so blue and significant that he forgot to breathe momentarily. Harvey schooled his features, needing to remain composed. He was a gentleman enjoying an evening with a beautiful woman, and that was all. No more or less than that, his wayward body needed to remember such things.

He pulled her close, the scent of roses teased his senses.

Even after all his warnings to remain aloof, he could not help but enjoy having such a woman in his arms. Beautiful, outspoken, a little absurd, but strong of will.

What was there not to like about her?

The top of her head came to just beneath his eyes, and he realized that she fit him perfectly, and considering he was a tall gentleman, most women barely made the top of his shoulders.

"You're taller than I thought you were," he said, mulling over whether he'd ever seen such a tall meg before.

She met his eyes, and her brow rose in question. "And I suppose you're going to tell me that being a tall woman isn't ladylike, along with me traveling north without a chaperone?"

He would not tell her that his thoughts were quite the opposite, regarding her height at least. But that response would not be appropriate for an unwed lady such as herself.

"On the contrary, it is refreshing having not to stoop so much when dancing."

A rosy hue kissed her cheeks, and she almost looked embarrassed by his compliment. "I was told only recently that I would appear much more genteel if I did not resemble a tree," she said. "I thank you for the compliment."

Harvey pulled her closer still, hating that anyone could speak to another without thinking about their feelings. Miss Hall was a beautiful woman, and whether he wanted her as a wife or not, which he did not, he repeated in his mind that he would not allow her to think otherwise regarding her beauty.

. . .

Evie remembered the night Lord Bourbon had proposed and his odd remark regarding her height. How was it her fault that his lordship had been the same height as she? Now, she could not help but believe Lord Bourbon's words weren't meant to be anything but mean-spirited. She had been self-conscious when towering over her friends and acquaintances from that moment. Did they think the same as Lord Bourbon? Did she look awkward when dancing and partaking in conversation? Did she truly resemble a tree?

"You, Miss Hall, do not resemble a tree. I can assure you of that," he said, his hold on her back tightening at his words.

Evie stepped closer still, wanting to revel in the heat of his nearness, the scent of his cologne that reminded her of leather and spice. Gosh, his lips...so perfect and soft-looking. Had those perfect lips kissed many women?

She closed her mouth with a snap, not wanting to be caught drooling over His Grace's good looks. When Lord Bourbon had tried to kiss her, which she thankfully avoided, she could not help but shudder to imagine his lordship's thin, chafed lips upon hers. How had she married him? She was surprised she had not run away sooner.

"What do I resemble, husband?" she teased, enjoying their closeness.

His eyes darkened with an emotion she could not read, and her throat suddenly felt tight and dry. Even so, she could not look away from his magnetic stare.

A muscle worked on his strong jaw, and his perfectly straight nose flared a little as he thought about her question. "Do you truly wish to know? The words, once spoken, cannot be taken back," he warned, his face but a breath from hers.

Evie swallowed but nodded, needing to hear his thoughts, wanting so much more than that. Would he kiss her? Did he wish to? Would he state that he had never seen such a beautiful woman?

A dream, of course. She had once been of the class that danced around them now. If not even lower in station than these people. A servant, a woman without wealth or connections. It was only by chance that her life altered the way it did. A fact that Lord Bourbon had made mention of many times when discussing her lineage.

"I do wish to know. Enlighten me?" she asked teasingly, not wanting the duke to know how vital his reply was to her injured, deprived soul that had never been complimented.

"Very well, let me begin..." He paused. "You resemble..."

EIGHT

Harvey debated what to say. There was something about being close to a woman who intoxicated the mind with her beauty and sweet-smelling skin that led to disaster most of the time. He breathed deep, fought to control the rogue within him that growled with ideas on how to seduce the delicious morsel of a woman in his arms.

Instead, he spun her quickly, eliciting a squeal of delight. "You resemble a woman I cannot help but believe is running away." Her eyes widened at his words, and he raised his brow. Had he hit on a sensitive subject? "Tell me, Miss Hall, who or what sends you fleeing to the Highlands?"

She averted her gaze and raised her chin, and he knew whatever it was that would come out of her mouth would be an aversion, a half-truth.

"I told you why I'm leaving for Scotland. I wish for a different future than the one set out for me in England. There is no other reason other than that. You speak like you expect me to hide some dark, mysterious secret."

"Are you not?" he asked, before thinking better of it.

She frowned and stepped out of his hold. The moment she left his arms, a feeling of emptiness swamped him, and he regretted not telling her what he wanted to say. That she was one of the most handsome women he'd ever met. That he wanted to kiss her, hold her, seduce her to his bed.

"You're my escort, husband. Are you going to tell me everything about your life in Scotland? Do you have a wife?" she whispered to ensure privacy. "Children? A mistress, mayhap?"

Harvey fought not to endure the nausea that usually accompanied the knowledge that duke or not, no one wished to marry nobility when their finances were in such a pitiful position.

"I have none of those things. But that does not change the fact that you're traveling to Scotland, whereas I live there most of the year. So you are the mystery here, wife. Not I."

"I think you're trying to bait me into saying something that would please you and not necessarily be true. I'm going to find some wine. I'm parched."

She marched off, and for the next hour, Harvey stood to the side of the room and observed Miss Hall dance with numerous gentlemen, many of whom examined her as if she were a sweetmeat to be feasted upon.

When Miss Hall downed her third glass of wine, her cheeks pinkened, her bright, unfocused eyes telling Harvey she had indulged enough for one evening. He joined the bevy of gentlemen who had swarmed around her and placed her hand on his arm. "Gentlemen, my wife and I must bid you good night," he said.

Disappointed groans abounded at his words, and inwardly, he laughed at the fools. Not that he had much to amuse him. It was not as if he could return to the inn with Miss Hall and slip her into his bed.

"Truly, darling? Must we leave? I'm having such a jolly good time," she said, smiling at the men as if they were a dessert in need of tasting.

Harvey did not enjoy the emotion that followed his thought. "Alas, what I say is true. We journey north tomorrow and must depart. I wish you all a pleasant evening."

The men mumbled their disapproval but did not stop him from guiding Miss Hall away. Her steps back along the main village road slowed the closer they came to the inn. Harvey glanced down and noted her efforts were not straight, and her clutch on his arm was stronger than usual.

"Do you require assistance, Miss Hall? How many glasses of wine did you consume?" he asked, knowing full well the number was three.

She hiccupped and covered her mouth with her hand, shocked at her outburst. "Only one, I believe, but I feel quite unsteady, Your Grace, and everything is shifting before my eyes."

He bit back a grin and, without warning, bent down and hoisted her into his arms. Carrying her to the inn was much quicker in any case, and he did not want her to fall and injure herself.

"Your Grace, put me down. You cannot carry me to the inn. What will people think?"

He met her gaze and grinned. "That my wife is a little foxed, and I'm carrying her back just as a good husband ought. There is nothing untoward with that, is there?" he asked, enjoying her womanly curves.

She blinked several times before he felt her relax in his arms. "Very well, do as you please. But know that I can walk

47

perfectly well. I think you merely want me in your arms," she cooed into his ear.

The whisper of her breath sent fire through his blood. He turned his head to look at her, halting his steps. Their faces were but a feather width apart. He could all but taste her sweet lips. Noticed her eyes grew heavy with need.

"I will not deny having a woman in my arms is pleasurable, but I do this to keep you safe, not to seduce you."

Her mouth opened on a gasp, but she did not respond. Probably best, as he did not know if he would follow his own decrees and keep his hands to himself. Certainly not if she were to say that she welcomed his touch.

There would be no saving either of them then.

E vie did not know what had come over her, but teasing the duke was paramount. Her body, relaxed, warm, and very delightfully snug in the duke's arms, could stay there forever.

How strong he was, his muscled chest pressing against her side with each step, with each breath he took. He smelled as divine as he looked, and she had not missed the many admiring glances ladies had bestowed upon him at the ball. Each of them wondered who he was. What was his name? Where was he from?

Well, for this evening, he was married to her, a husband much nicer than the one she had run away from only days before.

When being held by him, the idea of being married to a kind man of similar character wasn't as heinous as she had thought it would be after Lord Bourbon.

He stepped into the inn yard, and only then did he place

her back onto her slippered feet. Evie held his arm as he led her into the inn.

How he oozed confidence and his certainty in the world. A common trait for people such as himself, when born so fortunate. She was not uncertain that the sea itself would not divide if he were to command it.

"Ah, my lord, you have returned. There is a small problem that I wish to speak with you about if you please," the innkeeper stated as they walked into the inn, the wobble in the older man's voice giving a glimpse into an issue more significant than he was leading them to believe.

"A problem?" His Grace stated, his features as unreadable as his tone.

She listened, wondering what the issue was with their booking. Oh, she hoped the inn still had a room available. Where would they stay if they did not? She did not want to spend a night on the carriage seat. If that were to happen, she may have to lean on the duke to gain an ounce of rest. The thought made her giggle, and the duke glanced at her, his eyes narrowing in deliberation.

"Ah, yes, unfortunately, my lord, with the village dance this evening, I'm afraid only one room is left. I have reached out to the other inns here in the village, and they're all full, so unfortunately, you will need to share a room this evening with your wife. I do apologize. I know this is not what you commanded I prepare for you."

"No, it is not."

Evie looked at the innkeeper and noted the slight sheen of sweat forming on his forehead. "It is of no consequence," she interjected. "We shall share a room, he is my husband, after all. It is that he snores, you see. Terribly so that I cannot sleep for trying. And in the morning, he is quite the gassy man."

The innkeeper gaped before he excused himself and shuffled off toward the kitchens.

His Grace turned and met her eye. "That was unnecessary. We do not have to explain why we do not sleep together, Miss Hall."

She shrugged, the room spinning a little at the motion. "Well, better to think I do not sleep with you because you're a snoring, fizzle-releasing husband than one who isn't actually my real spouse," she whispered.

"Come, it is time for you to go to bed." He snatched up the room key and pulled her upstairs.

Evie followed, daring not to go to bed as he ordered, and yet, the idea that he would forever be known at this inn as a fizzle-releasing, snoring gentleman did tickle her common heart.

CHAPTER

NINE

Harvey sat in a chair, staring at the fire, and fought to ignore the silhouette that teased him through the screen where Miss Hall currently stood. She was washing up after the village dance, and he could see her strip from her gown, pulling the dress over her body, revealing a delightful figure beneath that made his mouth water. It was not what he needed in his life.

Damn it all to hell.

He clamped his jaw shut and fought not to suggest they sleep in the same bed. He would stay here this evening, in this chair, and not anywhere else.

"Are you certain you're happy to sleep in that seat?" Miss Hall asked, coming out from behind the screen in nothing but her shift and a small shawl.

The shift was of good quality, all but translucent, and he stared at her naked feet and ankles for longer than he ought.

"I have slept in worse places, Miss Hall. I can assure you it is perfectly adequate."

"Not adequate for a duke, I would say." She bustled over

51

to the bed and climbed into the sheets. "Oh, they've left a warming pan in here. How delightful." She smiled at him with such delight that he wondered if she had ever encountered one.

"But I do worry that it may cause a fire. Can you remove it for me?"

"Of course," he would do anything if she only went to sleep and left him be. The sooner he stopped talking and having to look at the delectable little chit, the better. He lifted the bedding near the foot of the bed and reached in, only to clasp what was certainly not a warming pan handle.

Miss Hall squealed and jumped at his touch, which made his hand slide higher on her calf. He wrenched his hand away, searched again for the warming pan, and, having hold of the correct item this time, wrenched it from the bed and placed it near the fire.

He dared not look at Miss Hall, ignoring that her legs were as smooth and soft as he feared. He should not have ignored the allure of that barmaid several towns back. Had he taken the wench to his bed, he certainly would not have found Miss Hall as sensual as he did.

Liar...

He dismissed the word that floated through his mind and sat back in his chair, moving about to ensure he was comfortable. He could hear Miss Hall toss and turn about in the bed before she sat up and blew out the candle on her bedside table.

Harvey kept his eyes closed, forcing them not to look and see what she was up to.

"The room is spinning," she murmured into the dark, which was only broken by the flickering lights of the fire. "I do not think I can sleep when I feel as though someone is spinning me about and I cannot make them stop."

His lips twitched at the notion that she was far more foxed than he first thought. "There is water beside your bed. Sip that and sit up a little to sleep. It may help you."

She did as he said, and without thought, he glanced at her. A mistake. She leaned against the wooden bedhead, the bedding laying atop her waist, all but leaving her breasts beneath her fine shift exposed through the transparent material.

Harvey swallowed, unable to look away as heinous as that was for a gentleman. Her breasts...

Well, he was certain he had never seen a lovelier handful in his eight and twenty years. His mouth watered, and his cock twitched in his breeches.

He'd always liked a good pair of breasts, and Miss Hall had quite the fine set.

"You are right. This is much better." A smile flittered across her mouth. How beautiful she was, her hair tumbled about her shoulders, her body in nothing but her unmentionables. For all the women of the *ton*, their expensive gowns and priceless jewels, as Miss Hall appeared before him at this very moment, that was true beauty.

E vie fought to keep her stomach contents where they should be and hoped the room would stop spinning. Not that she thought that would be anytime soon since it turned at quite an alarming rate and would not relent.

"I feel as though I'm going to fall off the bed, Your Grace," she said. "Even when I hold the bedding, it does not make me feel any less vulnerable."

He sighed, and the leather on his chair creaked before footsteps sounded across the wooden boards. Evie opened her eyes, a mistake, as the duke all but spun around her like they were on a tumbling ball.

The bed dipped at her side, and an arm slid behind her back, wrenching her toward the middle of the bed.

The notion that the Duke of Ruthven, Laird of Cheyne, was comforting her and keeping her safe from her indulgences left her mind reeling even more.

She laid her head on his shoulder, breathing deep and calm. "I'm so sorry to be a nuisance. You must be looking forward to being rid of me when we reach Aberdeen."

He chuckled as his hand made circular movements atop her shoulder. "I would be lying if I said that having to escort a lady was not troublesome, but I do not dislike you, Miss Hall, and so it is not so bad having to help you in your time of need."

She scoffed, wrapping her arms around his waist when the sensation of slipping engulfed her. "Has anyone ever told you how well you smell? Like sandalwood and spice. Delicious."

He stilled in her arms, and she held him tighter. "No," he said, clearing his throat. "They have not."

"Well, you do. I could smell you all day and never grow tired of it." She looked up at him and smiled. He did not return the gesture, but the light in his eyes burned with an interest she had only once seen in Lord Bourbon, and that was not when he was in her arms.

"I think you would be better off to rest now," he suggested, closing his eyes in an attempt to ignore her.

And yet, Evie knew instinctively, perhaps a woman's intuition, that he was very aware of her presence. "There were many ladies this evening who watched you, Your Grace. How unfortunate for you that this evening you had a wife," she teased, a shiver running down her spine when his finger started to run a line up and down her arm.

"Some would say you were the unfortunate one this evening, Miss Hall. To have a husband come and collect you when you were the flavor of the evening. I ruined your ability for amusement, and possibly true love."

She sighed heavily. "I do not believe in love, Your Grace. Do not fret on my behalf that I was injured by your presence. And in any case, you were the most handsome man at the dance, so I was most fortunate indeed." The words slipped from her lips before she could wrench them back. She snuggled into his side, hoping he would put her wayward mouth down to being foxed.

He was handsome, yes, terribly so and so alluring, but he was also a stranger. Her escort, duke notwithstanding. She was not looking to marry again unless, this time, she loved the gentleman, trusted him above everyone, and knew to her very core that he was a good man.

"Sleep now, Miss Hall, before you say another word that you do not intend. Not that you will remember a word uttered, which is likely most fortunate for you come morning."

"So long as you hold me until the room stops spinning, Your Grace, I shall be blessed indeed." Evie snuggled closer. The warmth of his skin, the *thump thump thump* of his beating heart against her ear, lulled her into a calmness she had not felt for some weeks.

In his arms, she felt protected and safe. That he proved he would not leave her or allow her to be hurt only made him so much more likable. But would he like her if he knew her true self? Not the fashionable lady she had been in London, but the common housemaid from Brighton who once served people such as himself?

Well, that was not entirely true. She served the middle class, people who were not even gentry, but worked in trade. Never would she have aspired to serve within a ducal estate.

She really ought to tell him how she came to be where she was, not just now in his bed, but the inheritance that plucked her out of a life of servitude.

Would he favor her then?

She did not think so. Not one of them would have given her a second regard. Lord Bourbon, even when betrothed, had often remarked on her common past. A dark cloud on his family he was willing to overlook due to her being related to Lady Lupton-Gage and an heiress. A blight he would never allow her to forget.

Would the duke think the same when faced with the truth? Only time would tell.

CHAPTER

TEN

Harvey woke with a start at the featherlight touch that tickled over his abdomen and settled on his hip. The feeling was accompanied by a sweet, feminine sigh and a warm, pliant body snuggled into his side, one leg haphazardly thrown between his.

He swallowed.

Hard.

He glanced down, unsure how he had come to be in this situation, and to confirm his worst fears. Miss Hall, with a satisfied smile on her lips, used his body as her cushion.

Her eyes closed, and her heavy sleep told him she had no idea her actions. But he did.

All too achingly aware of her touch, body, and sweet scent.

Damn.

He dared not move, not wishing to startle her. He doubted the guests at the inn would welcome a young lady screaming down the place as if something untoward was occurring.

Which, of course, it was not. He had not touched a hair on her head.

Harvey lifted his hands away from them both, not daring to move, lest she wrap herself even more around him. The urge to pull her close made his fingers twitch. Would she kiss him back if he brushed her sweet, pouty mouth with his? Seduce her to be wicked with him?

She let out a little snore, and he bit back a laugh. He'd never contemplated a woman asleep. Not to say he had not slept with a woman, merely had not taken the time to remain and indulge in the action for a full night.

After sleeping with Miss Hall, he had to admit the pastime of having a woman beside him in bed could have its blessings.

"Oh, I do not wish to wake from this dream," she moaned.

Harvey closed his eyes, not needing to hear her seductive, sleepy tone. Whether for him or not, his reaction to her voice was visceral.

With her words, Miss Hall lifted her leg, placing her sex against him. He dared not move as she undulated against his thigh, her hand sliding over his chest, pulling him close.

His cock sprung to attention, his mind unable to inform his second head that there would be no morning fuck. No matter if Miss Hall's body in sleep wanted otherwise.

He felt the moment she startled awake. Her body froze, stiffened with the knowledge that she was dry-humping his leg.

With a slow, torturous reality, she glanced up and met his eyes.

"Your Grace...I ah..."

He threw her a small smile and reached down, removing her leg from between his and rolling her onto her back beside him. "Good morning to you too, Miss Hall." He threw back the bedding and climbed out, ignoring the startled squeal as Miss Hall noted his nakedness.

He turned, not bothering to cover himself or his raging hard-on. She had humped him to the point he wanted to clasp his cock and join the fun, and so she would have to deal with it.

"I always sleep naked, Miss Hall, but I assure you, you were quite safe with me. On the other hand, my reputation may have been compromised had I stayed in bed a moment longer with you."

She huffed out an insulted breath. "I hope you are not insinuating anything, Your Grace. I would never have crossed any boundaries we agreed to. I merely found myself wrapped in your arms, a likelihood that is always possible when a couple sleeps in the same bed. I assure you I did nothing with your body as you insinuate."

"Really?" He grinned, pulling up his breeches and tying the falls. She glanced down, and her shoulders slumped. Had the little English lass enjoyed the view and was disappointed he had shoved her interest away?

Intriguing...

"Of course. I do not know what you think I was doing, but I assure you I was proper and remained dressed. Unlike some people now standing in this room."

She climbed out of bed in a temper and rounded on him. Harvey forgot in an instant what he was teasing her about as her breasts bounced with every move. Her nipples were as clear as the daylight coming through the drawn curtains, making their presence known in her all-but-translucent shift.

Blast the woman. She was a goddess and, damn it all to hell, one he wanted when he should not.

. . .

"I cannot believe you would think I would wish to seduce you. That was not my intention." Evie crossed her arms at the duke's fixed gaze riveted on her. She glanced down and wished the ground would open up and take her forever.

Her shift, which she thought proper, was all but diaphanous. Did that mean he could see everything? She reached for her shawl, covering herself as best she could, and fought not to die of embarrassment.

Of course, what he said was true. She had woken to such an erotic dream that it could be nothing else but that term. Not that she knew what her body was experiencing, but the thumping ache made her breath catch, and a longing arose between her legs, and would not repent.

She had dreamed of the duke. She had wanted to touch his person and enjoy every morsel that made up his magnificent form, and in her dream, she supposed she had transferred that need by touching His Grace in the bed.

She had undoubtedly woken to the notion that she had been undulating against his thigh like some hussy. It had taken all of her strength not to crawl up his body and make him show her what it was, the feeling overtaking her, having him touch her and satisfy her craving.

She closed her eyes, savoring the memory, and fought to remain calm, the woman she was supposed to be now that she was an heiress. A woman who did not misbehave, not regarding her reputation and virtue.

The duke stood across the other side of the bed, naked from the chest up. Never would she be the same, knowing what he looked like under those snug breeches he now wore.

The size of his manhood was large. As innocent as she

was, even she could discern that. But its hardness, with a slight upward curve, appeared as if it were seeking its mate, which was not what she had thought to see. Did the duke want her? Had her touch made him react so?

Would such a phallus even fit in her body?

The idea made warmth pool at her core, and she shivered. Pity she would never find out, not with the duke at least.

"I may not have been your intention, but your body certainly wished to fuck me," he blurted, his Scottish brogue even more pronounced in the morning.

Fuck? She had never heard the term before and frowned. "I do not know what you remark, Your Grace."

He chuckled and came around the bed to stand before her. The scent of sandalwood teased her senses, and she fisted her hands at her sides lest she reach for him.

Tension filled the room, ready and poised, and something told her that if she touched him, ran her hand over his chiseled chest, or along his strong jaw, nothing would ever be the same again.

Touch him, Evie. To love is to live...

She fought the urge and remained unmoving.

"The word means that you wish for me to lay you on that bed, spread those long, delightful legs of yours, and sink my cock into your willing heat. Take you, again and again, fill and inflame you until you're clawing my back and crossing your ankles against my ass, fucking me in turn."

Evie shut her mouth with a snap. Warmth pooled at her core, and she fought the urge to fidget, move, and squeeze her legs closed to offer a little satisfaction. "I would never do that," she lied.

Oh, yes, she would do such a thing if he only would teach her how.

He chuckled and moved toward the fire, throwing logs onto the hot coals and stoking it. Warmth kissed her back, and she heard him go about the room, dressing.

Evie heeded his direction and moved to stand behind the screen for privacy. She dressed as quickly as her shaking fingers would allow and took several deep breaths, attempting to stop her racing heart.

She heard him ring for a servant, and before she had finished her morning ablutions, a maid had brought up an array of pastries and a hot pot of tea for her and coffee for His Grace, if the nutty, smoky scent were any indication.

"I have ordered you breakfast, Miss Hall. Come out from behind the screen and eat, and we shall go. I promise not to mention our morning petting session again."

She rolled her eyes and stepped from behind the screen, glaring at him. "I do not find what you say amusing. I did not wish to seduce you. I think you consider too highly of yourself, Your Grace." Evie ignored the kiss of heat on her cheeks as she poured herself a cup of tea and his knowing smirk that all but oozed with disbelief.

One thing was for sure: the Duke of Ruthven was no gentleman, for no such man would remind a woman of their failings or their pettings in sleep as he termed them.

CHAPTER

ELEVEN

J ust after luncheon, they arrived in the quaint village
of Wetherby. Having left Doncaster early in the morning, Evie had not felt like eating the breakfast the
duke had ordered, not after he accused her of trying to
seduce him. Her stomach had been in knots and breakfast
was the last thing on her mind. The embarrassment that
plagued her after her lack of control in the bed they shared
had made her stomach unsettled—a mistake she now
understood. For the entirety of the journey, her stomach
had not stopped rumbling, and she was now feeling quite
faint.

The duke pulled the carriage to a halt before the inn, a
wooden-framed building that looked in need of several
repairs. Evie jumped out of the carriage and took a satis-
fying breath of fresh air. The closer they traveled toward
Scotland, the cleaner and crisper the air smelled. London
had been full of coal smoke, and one could not even see the
sun for half the days.

"Are you ready for luncheon?" the duke asked, holding
out his arm.

"I am, yes." She took his arm, hoping he had forgotten her morning faux pas. The duke barked out orders to the stable hands to water and rest the horses. Two young men ran around to do his bidding.

Upon entering the building, he handed the innkeeper two gold coins and asked for a meal. Without delay, they were ushered into a private parlor where trays of roast meats, bread, cheese, and delicious wine were soon brought in for them.

"This looks appetizing," she said, smiling across the table at the duke.

The slow lifting of his lips made her stomach clench, and she averted her gaze, not wanting him to see how much he affected her. And oh dear, he dissembled her more with each day that passed, especially after what she had done to his leg just hours before.

Ever since, her mind had been bombarding her body with feelings she had not known existed—a vexing and confusing dilemma.

Their night alone had been one of the most erotic moments of her life, even though she had not done anything to His Grace, nor he to her, and yet, she could not stop pondering it.

A maid brought in another tray of sliced lamb. "If you will, my lord and lady, there is a town fair today if you're looking to break your journey. It is but a few minutes' walk from here."

"A town fair?" Evie said, having never been to one of those before. "Do you think we can attend, Your... husband?" she corrected, having almost blurted his title aloud.

Traveling incognito, it would never do to announce who

the duke was or that he was traveling with a woman without a chaperone who was not his wife.

The maid dipped into a curtsy and left them alone. "If you wish, but it will mean we will not make Boroughbridge this evening as planned. We shall have to stay here."

"I do not mind if you do not." Evie placed several pieces of sliced beef and chicken onto her plate and poured hot gravy over it all. Her stomach rumbled again, and the duke laughed.

"I will remember to pack a basket of food for our travels when you refuse to eat breakfast. We cannot have you so famished."

Evie took the first bite of food and agreed she had never tasted anything so good. "It was my fault. I should have eaten this morning." And not let his teasing earlier get the better of her.

Without warning, the duke leaned across the table and, using his finger, ran it along her chin to her lip. He sat back in his chair, meeting her eyes as he slipped his finger into his mouth and sucked it clean.

Everything in Evie stilled. She felt her mouth gape as he licked his finger clean of whatever it was he wiped from her face. His eyes burned with mysterious intent, and she did not know what to do. Instead, she lifted her napkin and dabbed her mouth, unsure what was happening.

"You had a little gravy on your face."

And you thought to remove it...

He sipped his coffee as if what he had done meant nothing. Evie concentrated on eating the remainder of her meal, fighting the urge to test him on that theory.

Not that she had to wait long. After several minutes of enjoying the delicious fare the inn supplied, the duke's bottom lip housed a little breadcrumb that refused to move, even as he chewed.

Evie stood, wanting to see how he felt when unceremoniously touched as he had handled her. Taking a chance, wanting to taunt him as he did her, she cupped His Grace's jaw and wiped the little crumb from his mouth, ensuring her thumb ran the entire length of his bottom lip. His eyes flashed with need, and desire coursed through her in turn.

You're playing a dangerous game, Evie...

"You had a little crumb on your lips, Your Grace," she whispered.

They remained where they were for several breaths, their heartbeats so rapid, Evie was sure they could hear them. His eyes narrowed and snapped to her lips, and Evie dared not move, scared he would do something. Or nothing at all.

Please, do something, she wanted to scream.

And then he did, and nothing, she was certain, would ever be the same.

H arvey did not know what came over him, but he could no longer deny the burning attraction between them. Hot and untameable, he stood, his chair clanging to the floor behind him.

He ignored the sound, his focus wholly on the woman before him. Her eyes widened, a longing burning within her blue depths that begged him to kiss her. Her lips parted with a soft gasp of expectation.

Did she see, sense what he longed to do?

He pushed several dishes aside and lifted her, settling her onto the table. Without fear, without a word of protest, her fingers spiked into his hair, pulling him against her with a fire that stoked his own. Finally, he tasted those succulent lips, drank from them, and relished having her in his arms.

They came together in a kiss that left his mind reeling. She tasted of gravy and wine, warm and welcoming like the meal. He took her lips in a savage embrace, one that said all that he could not voice.

I want you. You make me so mad with desire that I cannot think straight.

Her tongue tangled with his, and his cock hardened. He stepped between her legs, her gown making it challenging to get close, but it would do for now.

"Evie," he moaned when her hand slipped down his back to cup his arse. She pulled him against her, taunting and frustrating them both with the restriction of their attire.

He reached for her gown and shuffled it up to pool at her waist. He would not take her, of course. He would never do such a thing to a maid, but he had to touch her. Tease her sweet flesh.

She was warm and, oh, so wet between her folds. He ran a finger along the opening of her sex, making sure to roll his thumb against her engorged nubbin.

She gasped, clutching at him, throwing her head back in satisfaction when he continued to tease her, play with her.

"I'm going to make you shatter in my arms, Evie. Have you ever come before?" he asked, his tone unlike one he had ever heard before, gravelly and uneven with need.

"No, never." She bit her bottom lip, and he covered hers, needing to taste her, to swallow her screams when he made her shatter in his arms.

Harvey did not know what came over him, but he had to finish what they had started.

He slipped one finger into her warm heat, his body roaring with desire as she used her arms as support and undulated upon his finger. All thoughts of her riding his cock just so bombarded his mind, and he fought not to spend in his breeches.

Blast and bless her. He'd never witnessed anything so sensual in his life. But it wasn't enough. He wanted more. So much more.

But what, without taking her here and now?

Harvey sat on the chair, hoisted her to the edge of the table, and covered her sex with his lips, sucking her, plying her little nubbin with his tongue until it wept and pinkened from his kiss.

"Harvey," she begged, using his given name for the first time. His cock pressed against his breeches, the sound of his name spilling from her lips almost severing his self-control.

"You taste so sweet. I could eat you all day," he admitted, in truth, having wanted to have the woman in his arms from the moment he had seen her defiant and strong-willed, driving a carriage alone to Scotland.

She was one of the most beautiful women he'd ever met. The least he could do was make her come on his face.

He groaned at the thought, pressing a finger deep within her while suckling her nubbin, lashing her with his tongue. She clutched his hair, pinning him against her, and he could feel the tension radiating throughout her body. Her legs shook, and tremors ran through her before she screamed through her release, begging him not to stop. To kiss her and give her what she wanted.

Harvey only wanted to satisfy her. He kissed her, deep

and long, wringing out the last of her pleasure until she was limp in his arms.

He stood, savoring her taste on his lips and knowing it would be too many hours before he did that again.

"I do not know what it was you just did, but know this, Your Grace. I will want it again, and until we part ways, you will give it to me, for it may be the only time I ever experience such joy."

He grinned, more than happy to oblige. "Of course, you are my wife, are you not? My only duty is to please you."

She grinned back. "Yes, I suppose I am until Aberdeen," she said, clasping his cravat and pulling him down for a kiss. Which he was also more than happy to oblige.

CHAPTER
TWELVE

Harvey could not stop brooding about what Evie
and he had done in the private dining room of
the inn only an hour or so ago. He stood before a
barrel of water full to the brim with apples and waited
for the local butcher to shout out the start of the absurd
competition he had agreed to.

Why was he partaking in the town fair, playing games
reserved for children? A question he did not want to
consider, not when he feared it might be because of the
pretty-faced lass who smiled and clapped several feet from
him, merely because he was taking part.

He was a duke. He ought to be lounging before a fire in
his room, drinking good whisky and thinking of how else
he could seduce the young woman who took up too much
time in his mind than she ought.

"Good luck, husband," Evie teased, smiling at him in a
way that made him want to drag her behind one of the
thatched-roof homes and have his way with her.

Would she allow such liberties?

He needed to cool his heels. She was a maid under his

care until Aberdeenshire. To touch her any more than he already had needed to stop unless he was willing to offer her his hand. Which he was not in the financial position to do.

"Go," the butcher yelled to them all.

Harvey dove under the water, determined to grab an apple with his mouth before anyone else, if only to end this torturous game. Getting one up against the side of the barrel, he bit into it. Just when he was about to crow to everyone in the contest he had won, a shout from a young girl beside him stole his win.

He stood with the apple in his mouth and couldn't help but laugh as the little girl jumped up and down, having won the game.

He met Evie's eye and smiled as she seemed to be wholly enjoying herself, witnessing him soaked from head to shoulder with a piece of fruit lodged in his mouth like a hog on a spit.

He grabbed the apple and rejoined Evie, eating it as he went. "Perhaps we ought to find a game for you to participate in? It's only fair since I went in the apple-bobbing one," he suggested.

She wrapped her arm about his, her breast brushing his arm as they moved away from the crowd that had come to watch. "If you insist, but I'm unsure what else they're doing."

Harvey looked around at the different games and spied one he knew he would enjoy watching. "There, that one over there that's about to start."

She looked over to where he watched, and her eyes widened. "That looks difficult and even more so if you're wearing a dress, which I am," she said, gesturing to herself.

He guided her over to the people preparing for the

event. "Come, it's only a cloth bag, and you need only to jump within it to the other side to win. I'm certain you can accomplish that."

"And if I don't, I end up in that mud instead," she said, giving the ground a look of disgust.

He bit back a laugh. "You will not fall any more than I drowned in that barrel full of apples. Come, it is only fair since I'm walking around this town drenched."

She sighed, and he knew the moment she conceded. "Very well, I shall take part."

He watched her go over to the gentleman running this event, who spoke to her for several minutes, no doubt explaining the rules, before handing her a bag to use. Within minutes, the jumping commenced, and Harvey found himself laughing harder than ever. Adults and children competed, yet the children seemed to have the game well worked out, while the adults struggled to get far, falling over, laughing too hard at their absurdness, and unable to keep their balance within the bag.

Evie was proving to be an exception, at least until she lost her balance and fell, landing flat in a muddy puddle.

Harvey ran to her and helped her to stand. He bit his lip, forcing himself not to react to her misfortune, and yet, her pretty face was covered in mud, little bits of straw, and several clumps of he did not know what. She opened her eyes and sputtered out whatever muck had landed in her mouth, staring at him in horror.

"I fell over," she said, as if unaware he already knew that fact.

His amusement fled at the vulnerability in her voice, and he wrapped his arm around her waist and helped her step out of the bag. He guided her out of the yard where the competition was being held and started toward the inn.

"Come, we shall return to the inn, and I'll have a warm bath prepared for you. It is unfortunate that you fell, but we shall have you clean and warm again in no time."

She wiped at the muck on her skin, the action pointless as it started to dry. "I think I swallowed some dirt," she muttered with disgust.

He cringed, hoping she did not become unwell. Who knew what festered in all the mud? "All will be well. I shall ensure a substantial dinner and wine. In no time at all, you'll be feeling much better."

She conceded but did not look convinced.

They arrived back at the inn, and heat kissed Evie's skin the moment the innkeeper and his wife's eyes widened at her disarray. Not that they would see her blush, for she was covered in muck from head to chest.

That the duke had seen her fall flat on her face and swallow earth that possibly contained horse excrement was a possibility she did not want to think about.

The innkeeper ushered them indoors and, without being asked, ordered a hot bath and whisky to their room.

Their room...

Before the duke could rectify the issue of their sharing, the innkeeper started up the stairs before them. "I took it upon myself, my lord, that since you attended the town fair, you would stay the night. I set aside one of our nicest rooms for you both. The bed has a new mattress and sheets and will be as comfortable as your own at home. Not to mention, the fire is alight, and all is ready for your arrival. If you're satisfied, I can have your luggage brought up at the same time as the water, if you will."

"Thank you," the duke said, giving the innkeeper a warm smile. "That would be very helpful indeed."

Happy with himself, the innkeeper left them alone, and it was only minutes before the bath was carried in, placed before the hearth, along with several buckets of steaming water for her use.

"I will try to wash my face in the basin first before my bath. I do not wish to bathe in the same water as what has dried on my face."

"Of course." The duke strode to the window and stared at the street. Evie went behind the screen and washed her face, feeling several small twigs threaded through her hair. When she was confident most of the grime was gone, she slipped out of her ruined gown and undergarments and wrapped a towel about her.

"I'm coming out now. Are you going to stay in the room while I bathe?" she asked, unsure if that was wise. The way he made her burn, what they had done in the private parlor downstairs only hours before, made her question seem moot, and yet...he ought to go. He wasn't her husband, and even though they had misbehaved, the duke had not been with her fully.

"Do you wish for me to leave?" he asked, his voice deep and reflective.

Evie walked out from behind the screen and studied his profile as he inspected the town go by outside the window. What was he thinking? Were his thoughts as jumbled and demanding as her own?

"Do you wish me to tell you the truth?" she asked.

He turned to look at her, his eyes dipping to the towel and lower still before settling on her feet. He blinked slowly and gave her his back. "Of course, always," he answered.

Feeling bold and wanting to throw caution to the wind,

Evie dropped the towel and stepped into the bath, sinking under the fragrant water that smelled of lemons. She dipped entirely under the water, rinsing herself as much as possible and hoping to remove whatever dirt she had missed in the basin.

Satisfied that she did not resemble a mud monster any longer, she hugged her knees in the tub and reveled in the duke's handsomeness. "Well, then, I would have to say that I do not wish for you to leave. In fact, I have never wanted anything more than for you to stay."

He sighed. In relief or despair, she could not say, but he turned, not averting his gaze, not even when she leaned against the back of the tub, gifting him full view of her body.

"We're playing with fire, Miss Hall."

She smiled and shrugged, unable to deny that they were. "Then I hope, Your Grace, I'm not the only one who gets burned."

THIRTEEN

S he was certainly not the only one who could be burned. Without thinking clearly or rationally, Harvey moved toward the bath, his body on fire, his heart thumping hard.

Damn, he wanted her. He wanted to fill her, take her, hear her moan his name as he brought her to release riding his cock.

She watched him, one eyebrow raised. Was she challenging him to join her?

He shrugged out of his jacket, laying it over a nearby chair. His cravat soon followed before he pulled his shirt over his head. Still, her eyes devoured his body like a physical caress. He wanted her hands on him. He wanted to experience her need for him, skin-to-skin.

"You cannot join me with your breeches and boots on, Your Grace," she teased, swirling the water with her hands, bringing his attention to her breasts that were in full view of him.

He took a calming breath, needing to keep his composure. He wasn't a green lad. He'd been with many women before, but something about making love to Evie was significant.

He wanted to ensure she enjoyed herself, found pleasure in his arms, and did not leave disappointed.

He ripped his falls open, kicked off his boots, and stripped himself bare. He stood before her, his cock rising to attention, and did not move. Allowing her to take her fill.

She bit her lip, and before he dared ask her to take him in her mouth, he stepped into the bath, sinking below the water to join her. Water sloshed over onto the floor, but he did not care, nor did Evie, who didn't say a word of protest.

She moved toward him, laying against his chest, her legs on either side of his hips. Her eyes burned with determination, igniting a fire within his soul before she closed the space between them and kissed him.

He groaned, having her in his arms once more, reveling in her lush, womanly curves against his rigid form. She was so soft and captivating that all his good senses fled.

"I could kiss you all day," she murmured, taking his lips in a kiss that stole his wits. Her tongue teased his and drew him ever nearer to losing control. How could he remove her from his life, drop her off in Aberdeen, and ride away? If only she were an heiress, a woman of his class, he could offer marriage.

As shocking as it was, the thought no longer scared him; only one part did, and that was her, living a life away from him.

"I'm here to oblige, wife," he teased, running his hand down her back, feeling a shiver alight down her spine.

She clasped his face and tipped it up to meet her eyes. "I want you to be my first, Harvey," she said, the sweet request leaving his head spinning.

"As much as we tease each other, there are risks if we're

intimate, Evie. Are you certain?" he asked, clamping his jaw closed and forcing himself to relax when she slid against his cock, teasing him unmercifully.

"Are there not things we can do to be safe?" she questioned.

He ran his hands along her back, clasping her ass and knowing he would do anything to have her tonight, but nothing was foolproof. "I can spend outside of you. That should hopefully alleviate any chance of a child." He paused, brushing his lips against hers. "I want to be your first too." And the last, but he could not say that. He was too deficient in his funds to offer her anything.

He rolled her against his aching cock and groaned. "You make me so hard." "Even when you fall in the mud, you're the most beautiful woman I've ever met," he acknowledged, unsure why he was being so honest, but knew, somewhere deep down, that he needed to be at least that with her.

"You make me feel things I never knew were possible." She lifted herself and slowly lowered her body onto his cock.

Harvey swore as she worked her way onto him, taking her time as he stretched her, filling her until he was cock-deep in her cunny.

She fit him like a glove, perfect and warm. "God, you feel good."

She held on to his shoulders and rose barely off him before coming back down. "Oh dear, that feels...very good indeed."

He half-chuckled, half-groaned, and leaned back against the tub, satisfied to allow her way, to watch her learn how to bring pleasure to herself using him, riding him, fucking him...

He had never seen any woman more captivating.

Evie remembered to breathe as she grew confident in lifting herself onto Harvey, having him fill and inflame her. He was a sizable man, long and thick, and having first seen his manhood, she had not been sure they would fit as they were supposed to.

But they had, and the fullness, the tremors he alighted within her with each movement was unlike anything she had ever experienced, a teasing motion, more potent than when he had placed his mouth on her sex and brought her to orgasm, as he named it.

His hands clasped her hips, guiding her, helping her to lift and inflame her with each stroke. Soon, she was in a pleasurable rhythm, but it was not enough; she needed more.

Evie leaned forward and clasped his face, kissing him deeply, her tongue mimicking what his manhood accomplished beneath the water. Never had she been so vulnerable, so forward as she was being with Harvey.

The first tremors of her orgasm ripped through her without warning, and she lost all conscious thought. "Harvey, do not stop," she begged, working against him like a woman possessed by need.

He did not disappoint, and the moment her tremors subsided, he lifted her from him and turned her about in the tub. "Brace yourself against the tub. I'm not finished with you yet," he growled, suckling his way along her spine.

Evie did as he suggested. The hairs on his chest tickled her back as he kissed her shoulder, his warmth enfolding her.

Expectation thrummed through her when he said,

"Bend over." His cock pressed against her bottom, slipping between her folds. Had he not found his release? Was he going to do more delicious things to her?

She waited with bated breath for whatever it was he wished to do. She would allow him anything at this point. Her heart thumped hard against her ribs, her skin bristling and sensitive to his every touch, the whisper of his breath against her cheek. Her cunny wept for more as if she had not just shattered in his arms.

What a wanton she was turning out to be.

"I'm going to make you come again. I promise you that." His Scottish brogue made her breath catch. He sounded deadly and full of promise.

He pressed on her lower back before she felt the pressure of his manhood slide into her sex.

So easy. "Ahh, so good," she gasped, reaching back with one hand to hold on to him, keeping him close.

He took her hand, placing it back on the tub. "You'll need to support yourself. I'm going to fuck you. Hard."

His words drew another shiver down her spine, and she quickly did as he ordered, unable to wait a moment longer. Not that she needed to, as he thrust into her.

"You feel so good," he moaned, taking her with a force that scattered her wits, her breath, her everything.

He took her with such need, such force that she cried out, the pleasure unlike anything she had ever imagined. His hand came around and cupped her cunny, his fingers working, rolling the sensitive nubbin that his mouth had suckled.

Evie did not know what to do or say. Her mind reeled as her body tensed, was taunted, and pushed toward another release that threatened to be far more significant than the last.

Her skin heated, her breath caught, and her breasts rocked as he took her from behind.

"I'm watching my cock take you. Fill you. Such a beautiful sight," he growled, his relentless strokes never giving way to anything else.

"Yes," she panted, pressing back against him, riding him as best she could, wanting to please him as he pleased her. He was so big, filling her, each stroke teasing a special little place within her that cried out for more.

And he gave her more. So much that she did not know where he began, and she ended.

Perhaps they did not. Maybe they were already one...

His hand rolled against her sex just as he thrust, and pleasure rocked through her. She heard herself scream his name, her body with a mind of its own, heedless of its actions, shattered into a million pieces.

"God, Evie," he gasped as his manhood hardened further, thickened in her heat before he wrenched free of her, his cock pressing against her bottom as warmth tickled her back.

He pumped against her, his release as all-consuming as hers, and she felt him tremble as his pleasure ebbed and slowed. They lay in each other's arms for several minutes, content to allow the warm water to soothe their overheated skin and beating hearts.

"I'm never going to get enough of you now that I've had you," he said, kissing her temple.

Evie hoped he would not. She could see herself in his arms for the rest of her days and happily, if he could bring her such pleasure. What woman would not want such a lover?

"That is satisfactory then," she said, spinning in the water and laying on his chest. "Because you have no complaints from me if you do."

FOURTEEN

T he next several days were a whirlwind of grueling travel and sensual nights in Harvey's arms. Through the villages they traveled, she was his wife, and Evie could not remember a happier time in her life.

But with each day that passed, so too did the nagging fear that she was being untruthful to His Grace. He thought her a woman of the genteel class who sought a life outside of Society and London. Not a woman running from a husband who refused to be faithful, even on their wedding day. What would he think of her truth? How would he react when he found out that she had once been a maid, a woman of such a low class that he would not have looked at her twice?

Evie stepped from the carriage with a sense of awe when they pulled up before a sizeable medieval castle with towers and battlements and an old moat that was still filled with running water.

"This is Cardell Castle, the Laird of Cheyne's seat here in Scotland."

She turned around in what she supposed was the bailey and took in Harvey's Scotland home. Never had she ever seen anything so grand, so old and powerful. Intimidating, if she had a word for it.

"It is unexpected, Your Grace," she said, using his title as servants and stable hands went about unhitching the horses and carrying their luggage inside.

"The hour grows late, so it would be best to remain here for the evening. I will drive you into Aberdeen tomorrow and help you secure a cottage or small manor house of your liking."

Evie fought not to let the disappointment show on her features. Their separation was bound to happen, and she had been preparing herself to be removed from him from the moment they came together. He had not offered marriage, and even if he had, she could not accept. Not until Lord Lupton-Gage sorted out her annulment from Lord Bourbon as she had asked.

She turned and studied the land surrounding the castle. Trees and valleys as far as the eye could see, a small, winding river made its way through the landscape, and yet above it all sat Cardell Castle, as grand and commanding as its owner.

"How lucky you are to have all of this. I do not think I would ever wish to leave Scotland should I live in such an inspiring place."

He took in her words, his surroundings, the landscape, and the building as if seeing it for the first time. "Aye, it is grand. I agree with you there, but it's an awful lot of work. Not to mention, it can be horribly cold in the dead of winter." He paused, throwing her a small smile. "And let's not forget, most of the ancestors that came before me still make their presence known."

A shiver ran down Evie's spine, and she frowned. "Are you trying to scare me, Your Grace? Or perhaps you do not wish for me to stay after all?" Evie swallowed, not so worried about whether the castle had ghosts, but the thought of leaving Harvey was more terrifying than anything else.

I'm not ready to part from you yet...

He grinned and did not answer her question. "Come, mayhap you will be welcome and they will leave you alone."

With trepidation making her heart beat hard, she followed the duke inside and left the stable hands and footmen to bring in their luggage.

The hall was no less grand than the exterior. Although the rushes that long ago covered the flooring were now replaced by large, square flagstones blanketed with thick rugs. There was a roaring fire at the center of the room, multiple tables, and an opulent chaise longue. "What is this room?" she asked, walking into the center of it and spinning about to take it all in. Tapestries depicting ancient clan warfare covered the walls, and yet still, the room had a chill she imagined would remain no matter how hot the fire or strong the attempt to make it cozy.

"This is the great hall. Meals were held within this space for past lairds and their clansmen. I have kept the tables in the room, and dinners are held here occasionally, but mostly it's for sitting before the fire and keeping warm. We also host balls in this room, but clear it of its furniture when we do."

"It would be a perfect space to hold such entertainment." Evie walked over to the fire and put her back to it, seeking warmth. "Do you hold many balls here?"

"No," he said, "but I should like to when it is feasible to do so."

Evie wondered what that meant, but she let it go when he sent a footman away for a plate of dinner for them both. He likely had reasons he did not entertain, the grounds of which he did not have to explain to her.

"How many rooms does the castle have? Have you ever counted them all?"

He joined her at the fire, standing as she did to warm his body. "You know, I never have, but I probably should. I'm certain there are rooms that I do not even know exist."

"Rooms that may have hidden treasures," she teased, excited by the prospect of looking about the castle before she remembered that would not be a ladylike thing to ask.

"You're welcome to explore before I take you into town tomorrow. I have some work to do with my steward, and we will break our fast before I take you into Aberdeen after lunch, if that would suit you."

Evie could hardly wait to start exploring. "I would like that very much, thank you." She reached out and touched his arm, needing to feel him, hoping that even with their parting, he still wished to be with her. "Thank you again for escorting me here, Harvey. You have been very kind, and I hope we may be friends even after I leave. I have enjoyed our time together, no matter what our futures hold."

"I would like that also, Evie," he whispered, dipping his head to steal a quick kiss, which solidified in her anxious mind that there was still hope for them.

.   .   .

Harvey fought the uneasy feeling that ran through him at the thought of leaving Evie in Aberdeen. Although only two miles from Cardell Castle, it may have been a hundred, so distant it felt.

He did not like the idea of her sleeping so far away from him or not in his bed where he could protect her. He thought of telling her of the financial troubles that plagued him. Would she understand why he could not offer marriage? Did she even wish him to declare himself to her? Was she hoping he would?

The thought of marrying an heiress to save his impoverished ass after being with Evie left a sour taste in his mouth, and he was relieved when a footman entered the hall carrying a tray of ham, cheese, freshly baked brioche, tea, and coffee, his favorite beverage.

"We shall eat before the fire this evening," he suggested, waiting for the footman to place the tray of food on the small table before the chaise and leave them alone.

Evie sat and poured herself a tea and him a coffee. "This looks appealing," she said. "I'm not sure about you, but I'm famished."

Pleased she was enjoying the fare, he smiled. How beautiful she was, sweet-natured, and often quick-witted. He had not thought to meet a woman on the north road such as her, but he was glad he had. What a breath of fresh air she was in his otherwise stale life.

The sound of a tree scraping the window's glass panes caught his attention, along with the heavy rain that tapped the glass in a sporadic dance. The Scottish weather was known to be changeable, but he hoped it did not rain too much to make traveling to Aberdeen difficult.

"Would you care to explore the castle with me after our

meal, Harvey? I should hate to get lost or go into a room I should not."

He bit into a fresh piece of ham and chewed. "I suppose I can indulge you this afternoon. I have no previous engagement, and since it has been some months since I've been home, it would not hurt to inspect the castle and ensure all is as it should be."

"Wonderful," she said, her blue eyes bright with excitement.

They ate for several more minutes, enjoying the great fare and warmth of the fire before he could not consume another bite. "Right, Miss Hall, what would you like to see first? The dungeons?" he teased, dropping his tone in an attempt to frighten her off.

Her chuckle made his heart stir. "Oh yes, I did not know the castle had a dungeon. Do please take me there and tell me everything you know about who was once captured and held here."

He took her arm and led her out of the great hall and toward the back of the castle, where the stairs leading down to the dungeons were positioned. Several servants glanced at them in bafflement as he escorted Evie toward a location where rarely anyone ventured.

"The cook refuses to go down here, even though the wine is housed in the space. She believes it's haunted by a one-armed man who likes to caress women's hair."

Evie's steps faltered, and he felt the tension in her hold. "Now, you must be teasing me. Tell me that is not true, for I'm not sure even I wish to go down there now."

He guided her down the stairs, not deterred by her fear. "Do not worry, Miss Hall. I'll protect you."

"Somehow, that does not make me feel any safer, even if you are the laird of all this."

Harvey picked up a lit sconce from the wall and made their way into a long corridor that appeared to go on for miles but, in reality, only several feet. "Just up ahead, the corridor spreads into a circular room with five cells positioned off from that. I do not know who may have been imprisoned here, but there are still shackles on the walls, and each room has a lockable iron door. It would not have been comfortable for anyone had they been imprisoned. No light penetrates the space."

Seemingly not soothed by his holding of her hand, Evie stepped against his side and snuggled under his arm. What was it about this woman that he enjoyed keeping her safe, wanting to comfort her?

Wanting her in all ways...

He held her close, reveling at having her in his arms. They were playing a wicked, dangerous game, allowing temptations to lead them astray, but he could not stop.

"The hairs on the back of my neck are standing on end," she whispered.

Harvey lifted his arm and felt along her nape with his finger. "No hair is on end. You're perfect under my touch," he replied before he could stop himself.

She glanced up at him, her eyes wide, her mouth parted, perfect for kissing, and a raw and commanding hunger ripped through him. He leaned down, determined to continue the whirlwind, or whatever it was that was happening between them, just as the sconce doused and a deafening scream accompanied the blackness that engulfed them.

FIFTEEN

T hey were going to be killed by the ghostly man who haunted the dungeons, was Evie's first thought as darkness swallowed them in the pits of the castle. Followed by the unmistakable sound of laughter from the duke, whom she could not see but only feel as his body vibrated with amusement.

"Harvey, this is not funny. Stop laughing," she ordered, unable to hide the wobble of fear in her tone.

"Come, I know my way out and will lead you to safety," he said, his tone one of confidence.

Evie closed her eyes, not wanting to see any ghoul, and allowed him to guide her from the dungeons. Several feet along the passage, a glow bathed the lids of her eyes, and she opened them, relieved to see the upstairs light guiding them out of there.

"Perhaps you could show me the parts of the castle that are not below ground level. I'm not too proud to admit that I thought we would be attacked by the ghostly figure your cook is scared of."

"No one has had anything occur to them in the

dungeons for hundreds of years, and I assure you that you will not be the first to break that history."

A shiver ran down her spine, and Evie was glad to be back in the great hall and moving toward a staircase that went upward instead of down.

"I will show you to your room. It should be ready by now, and after dinner this evening, I will show you the rest of the castle. You must be tired and need rest after our journey."

Evie was unable to disagree, no matter how much she wished to take a tour. But she wanted to freshen up and inspect her room, even if she was fortunate enough to only sleep in it for a night.

The winding stone staircase brought them up to the first floor. A large landing divided the castle into two, leading off in separate directions. His Grace led her left and down a passageway, the long Aubusson rug attempting to give the impression of warmth. Yet, no matter how much the duke tried to modernize and seal the ancient walls from the wind and rain, a chilling draft blew through the corridors.

He stopped before a dark oak door with a metal handle and, opening it, swung it wide. "This is your room. You have windows on the east and south of the space, so there is much light throughout the day. We're high on the mountain, so trees will not impede your view."

Evie took in the space, the dark wooden furniture, the roaring fire, and the thick rugs underfoot. The windows gave a view of the valley below, and she could make out the river she had seen earlier winding through the woods. "The weather is atrocious. Do you think it will stop raining before I leave? I would so love to see the gardens."

He joined her at the window and took in his land. "I do

not know. The weather is so changeable here in Scotland, and this storm looks settled."

A flash of lightning and the rumbling of thunder did not bode well for her plans.

Harvey sighed. "If this rain keeps up, you may not get to leave tomorrow. The river rises quickly and takes several days to lower. I probably should have taken you straight into town."

The idea of remaining in the duke's castle should have filled Evie with concern. She was a maid and unchaperoned, for all they knew. What would the staff think? She supposed the duke would have given them some explanation as to her arrival or merely ignored their curious glances and let them think whatever they liked.

But did he not wish for her to remain? Had his interest in her waned already? Perhaps he did not have affection toward her, unlike what she was starting to feel toward him.

"I hope I have not caused you too much trouble, Your Grace," she said, feeling like a burden. After all, she had accosted and begged him to escort her to Scotland, and now she was being a pain and having to stay at his home.

He turned and reached for her, and her stomach did a little flip. "You have never been a burden, Evie. Do not think that having you here makes it so. I worry about your reputation. We are not playing by the rules." He kissed her forehead and let her go, striding from the room.

Evie reveled at his tall, muscled frame that drew the feminine eye and his concern for her welfare. Why was such a caring man not married? A virile, young duke such as himself ought to have a loving wife and children by now. Odd that he did not.

. . .

H arvey inwardly cursed and strode from the room. He made his way down the corridor past the staircase and toward his suite. He shook his head, cursing himself a fool for playing her as he was. He could offer her nothing. Not yet, at least, and he doubted she would wait, risk her reputation to be with him until he could afford to propose marriage.

Offer her a marriage now, and damn the debt.

He shuddered at the thought of bringing any woman into the world where one could not offer them the luxury that ought to come with a ducal title. What he shared with Evie was a passing fancy for them both. She had said herself that she was not looking for a husband. Wanted a life away from society.

Make her your mistress...

Harvey ripped off his cravat, throwing it on the bed. Before heading downstairs for dinner, his valet joined him and helped him change into clean breeches, a shirt, and a new jacket. Not that being refreshed helped to lift his mood.

His steps slowed at the sight of Miss Hall before the fire in the great hall, warming her hands. She studied the coat of arms hanging over the fire, her mouth open a little in awe.

He could understand being a little overwhelmed by this castle. It was immense, with so much history, the turrets, the great hall, a chapel, a drawbridge that no longer worked, so much to take in that left even him in wonderment at times.

"The cross is the Cheyne family crest. It means patience conquers."

She met his eyes, and he forced himself to continue

toward his study. "You are welcome to sit before the fire and rest a while. I have some work to attend to, but dinner will be served soon after, and I shall join you again then," he said, wanting to remove himself from her presence.

The more time he spent with her, the more he realized he did not want her to leave. He wanted her to share his bed and his life, but how, when debt hung over him like a curse? If he did not marry an heiress, his hope of marriage soon would not transpire.

The debt his father left him wallowing in would take years to get out of, and all the people who worked for him at his many estates deserved an income. An income he was finding more challenging to pay each month.

"But what about the tour you promised me?" She followed close on his heels into his office.

"I wish to go through some correspondence and then take you on a tour. Will that suffice?" He flicked through the many letters, one in particular, an invitation from Lord and Lady Roxborough, and his mouth dried.

"Is everything well, Harvey?" she asked, approaching him and placing a comforting hand on his arm. "You are being a little distant from me."

He threw the invitation down on his desk and schooled his features. "I'm sorry if you feel that way. I do not mean to be distracted." He gestured to the invitation on his desk. "I forgot that I'm to attend a dinner at the Roxborough estate not far from here this evening."

"Oh." She threw him a small smile and started to walk about his office. "Well, I shall leave you to your business. I'm sure I shall be well looked after by your staff until you return."

He did not like the disappointment in her features, thinking he would not include her. He scribbled a short missive before ringing a bell for a servant. "I shall send word that you'll be joining me. We shall say we know each other from mutual friends in London and that they asked me to help you settle in Aberdeen. They need not know that you are a guest at my estate this evening."

"Truly?" she asked. "But are you certain? I do not wish to intrude."

"If anything, you shall make the dinner a much more enjoyable evening than it would otherwise have been." A servant knocked on the door, breaking their solitude. "Please have this note delivered to the Roxborough Estate posthaste," Harvey ordered, not the least annoyed by the prospect of going out, even in the terrible weather. When did Scotland not deliver on that score?

"Whatever shall I wear? Do not ladies wear tartans in Scotland, or is that only what I have read in stories?" Evie leaned on his desk and looked at him as if he were some great wealth of information on women's attire.

He chuckled. "A dinner gown will be perfectly fine. But I shall supply you with a tartan shawl to keep you warm."

"Will I have met these people in London, do you suppose?" she asked.

He shook his head. "I do not believe so. It has been several years since Lord Roxborough has traveled south."

SIXTEEN

E vie dipped into a curtsy as she was introduced to Lord and Lady Roxborough, an elderly couple who seemed pleased by her attendance, and yet the sly look that passed between Lord Roxborough and His Grace made her curious.

"How wonderful to have you here, Miss Hall. Do come into the drawing room. We're having mead or wine, if you prefer, before dinner is served."

"That sounds wonderful, thank you." Evie followed Lady Roxborough, taking in the magnificent house, very different from the duke's yet just as grand. Similar to the Georgian home Lord and Lady Lupton-Gage occupied in London.

The drawing room was full of guests laughing and discussing whatever interested them. Evie had not thought that society would be so similar to that in London, but she could, for all the distance that separated her, be walking into a dinner party in England.

Evie felt the duke's presence following her, and she smiled at several people, hoping they would not exclude her and happy that she did not recognize anyone from London.

"Miss Hall, let me introduce you to Mr. and Mrs. Tonkin. They live in Aberdeenshire. Mr. Tonkin's son is our local vicar."

"Lovely to meet you," Evie said, relieved when Harvey commenced a conversation regarding the weather and saved her from any awkward silences.

"So, my dear. You're from England. What brings you up to the Highlands?" Mrs. Tonkin asked, her eyes wide with interest.

Evie could not disclose the truth and remembered what His Grace had said they would say. "I wished to see if Scotland would suit me as a place to live. His Grace, a friend of a friend in London, has been good enough to include me this evening. But I hope to find a small manor house soon to lease or buy so I may live here."

Lady Roxborough and Mrs. Tonkin both stared for several heartbeats before Lady Roxborough broke the silence. "You mean to live in Aberdeenshire alone..."

"I shall have a maid, lady's companion, and a manservant, but yes, that is what I wish."

"Well, I never." Lady Roxborough looked to the duke, and Evie wondered if even that truth was too much for the elderly ladies.

"You cannot allow Miss Hall to live alone, Your Grace. You must write to her people and have them come to fetch Miss Hall. It would not be proper that she live alone, like an old maid, not when she could be married and have a family of her own."

Evie shook her head, unwilling to heed caution against one so set in their ancient ways. "I will be chaperoned, and I'm quite capable of living independently, Lady Roxborough. I do not need anyone to rescue me when I do not want them to."

"But you're so young and unmarried. The scandal of it all," Mrs. Tonkin gasped, clutching her large pearls around her neck.

Evie did not know what to say and looked to Harvey, who seemed equally shocked by the turn of conversation.

"Your Grace," a feminine voice broke in between their conversation. Evie inwardly sighed, pleased that another guest was joining them. Her relief, however, was short-lived when it was Lady Miller.

Evie fought to calm her rapid heart. What was Lady Miller doing in Scotland? The last time she had seen her was in London for the Season. What could possibly have brought her all the way to Aberdeenshire?

"Lady Miller." The chill in the duke's tone seized Evie's attention. She studied the duke and noted the tightening of his lips, the muscle in his jaw flexing. "I did not know you would be in attendance this evening."

"Did you not?" She chuckled, as if her response was amusing. "How fortunate we shall meet again. Before his passing, Lord Miller spoke of missing your company, so I thought to do what he could not and come to Scotland. It has been long overdue."

"Is that so?" The duke sipped his mead, disinterested.

"And Miss Hall?" Lady Miller eyed her, and the loathing that Evie read in her cool gaze set her heart pounding. So, Lady Miller did know who she was and remembered her.

Oh dear, Harvey would never forgive her if he found out the truth of her past. Her marriage.

"How lovely to see you again." Lady Miller took Evie's arm and entwined it with hers. "Let us take a turn about the room."

Without waiting for an answer, Lady Miller stepped past the duke and, before Evie could say no, whisked her away.

They promenaded for several steps, the silence growing deafening, to the point Evie was sure Lady Miller could hear the blood rushing through her veins.

"It is odd that you're here, and with the duke, especially when you have a husband in London that you just married. Does the duke know that you're playing him the fool?" Lady Miller asked, her tone sweet, her words bathed in threats.

"If you must know, the marriage will be annulled, my lady. I would prefer we not speak on the matter again this evening." Evie swallowed the fear that Lady Miller had no intention of letting her forget, and the smirk on her ladyship's lips only solidified her suspicion.

"The duke is not for you, my dear. For all your wealth, which I'm certain is tied up now with this foolish annulment that you wish to achieve, you are a servant at heart. I will be surprised you come out of this scandal of your own making without a reputation." The countess laughed, but there was no joy in the sound. "The duke has no money, you know. He is as asset rich and poor in every other way that counts. He requires an heiress to save his many estates."

"My money was not entailed with the marriage, my lady. Lord Bourbon, for all his vices, was rich. My money is mine to do with as I please."

Lady Miller raised her brows. "Well, Lord Lupton-Gage was intelligent to protect your inheritance, but answer me this, Miss Hall. Has His Grace asked you to be his wife? Has he declared his love that surpasses all his unfortunate money woes?" She chuckled. "Oh dear, I can see by your fallen visage that he has not."

"Can you?" Evie fought back the tears that swam in her

eyes. Hating that Lady Miller was right and that Harvey had not offered marriage. He thought her unattached, free to do as she pleased. Why had he not asked? Did he not feel as she did, as if her world had turned upside down the moment she met him?

"I wonder if he would ask you to be the next Duchess of Ruthven if he knew you were an heiress? Shall we go and speak to him? Perhaps you will be engaged even by the time you return to Aberdeen this evening. That is if he can wait for your annulment to be approved."

"His Grace knows nothing of my past. Please do not say anything, Lady Miller. He is a friend, and that is all." Evie pulled out of her hold, wanting to be as far away from this woman who encompassed everything she hated in London. The disloyalty, the false friendships, the women who married for money and status above love. "I thank you for your delightful conversation and turn about the room." Evie dipped into a curtsy just as the dinner gong sounded in the depths of the house.

The duke came up to her side, a small smile on his lips. "Shall we, Miss Hall?" he asked her, holding out his arm.

Evie met his eyes and saw his curiosity regarding their conversation, but she could not explain the interaction here, and certainly not now.

"Do you know Lady Miller well?" Evie asked as they moved into the dining room, wondering why the countess seemed so vicious. What was it to Lady Miller who the duke arrived at a dinner party with? They had been acquaintances in town but never enemies as they seemed to be now.

"I was engaged to Lady Miller before she married the earl. He was a friend, and when she found out that I..."

"That you what?" Evie asked when he did not elaborate.

"Well, she informed me her affections were elsewhere and married the earl instead. Although I did not think so then, it was good for us both. It was not a love match."

Evie studied him a moment before he stopped in front of a chair and helped her to sit. Something told her he had been about to say something else before changing his mind.

But she would have to wait until they were alone before asking, although she had a little inkling as to what it could be.

SEVENTEEN

T hankfully, the remainder of the dinner was uneventful, and bidding Lord and Lady Roxborough goodnight, Evie took Harvey's hand as he guided her into the carriage.

She settled back in the opulent velvet squabs and placed her slippered feet on the warming bricks the coachman had placed there for them to use. This evening, the drive back to the duke's castle would be slower due to the weather, and yet, with the fur-lined cloaks sitting on the seats, their journey would be pleasant and comfortable.

She sat across from Harvey, appreciating him in his fine evening wear, his superfine coat and silver waistcoat beneath that sat a kilt. He looked perfectly Scottish and so very handsome. He never failed to make her stomach flutter with nerves.

"I hope you found the evening entertaining." He settled a cloak over her legs before easing back in the seat. "I know some people can be a little too much."

"I suppose you mean Lady Miller." Evie shook her head, thankful her ladyship had not disclosed her knowledge of

Lord Bourbon in London to the duke. But Evie knew she had to tell him soon. Tomorrow, before she left, she would explain everything that occurred on her wedding day and hope that he would forgive her.

Lord Bourbon was her husband, but soon, that marriage would be annulled, and everything would be right in the world. Lord Lupton-Gage would not let her down. She was sure of it.

"You looked very beautiful this evening." He threw her a small smile that always made her feel warm and safe. There was something about this man that she never wanted to be parted from.

They may not have started the best of friends; the circumstances were odd indeed, but he had become one of the people in her life whom she thought most highly of and cared for so very much.

Did he care for her? Or were his financial woes greater than what his heart desired?

Not that she knew if he desired her in that way. She may be nothing but a passing fancy for the duke, but she could not see him treating her with such little respect. It did not suit his character.

No. Lady Miller had to be wrong, maybe not about his financial position, but his nature.

How long are you willing to wait to test that theory? As Lady Miller suggests, what if he never proposes and marries an heiress?

Evie pushed the unhelpful thoughts aside. "You are so far away. Why do you not come here, and we can share the fur blanket."

The wickedness that burned in his eyes at her suggestion sent her heart racing, and she flipped back the fur rug and chuckled when he came and sat beside her. He tipped up her face to look at him, and at that moment, Evie knew she was in trouble.

Her heart certainly was. She longed for him to propose, offer her a future brighter than she had ever imagined. A love match on her behalf, at least, that was paramount to her future happiness.

Please ask me to marry you before you know I'm an heiress so I know your heart is true...

His lips brushed hers, the softest touch, and longing ripped through her, sending her wits to spiral and all thoughts of proper behavior to go with them. Evie threw the blanket to the floor and straddled Harvey, having missed him these past two days as they traveled to Scotland.

She needed him. Needed to know that he desired her, wanted her as much as she wanted him.

"I want you," he growled, his voice deep and thick with the Scottish accent.

Evie worked her gown out of the way. He did the same for his kilt, and like a frenzy of hands and rapid breaths, Evie joined with him, sinking low on his manhood, which filled her with exquisite pleasure.

He was so hard, big, and she stilled a moment, needing to calm herself, wanting to prolong their joining.

But it was no use. He thrust into her, taking her breath, her wits, with every stroke.

How was she going to leave tomorrow? Move to Aberdeen, if only a few short miles from Harvey? How could she not fall asleep in his arms every night?

Please love me as I love you...

"I want you too." Evie wanted to say so much more. Tell him everything he needed to know, not just of her past, but of her heart and how it only beat for him.

He lifted her from the seat and lay her upon it, coming over her again. Evie wrapped her legs around his waist, reaching for him. She kissed him deep and long.

"You drive me to distraction. I forget what is right and wrong when I'm with you."

She could understand his words. Hers mirrored his. So much to say and so much hidden at the same time. Evie bit her lip as the first tremors of her release rocked through her.

He thrust into her and gave her what she wanted before she spiraled over into a kaleidoscope of delight. Her body rocked against his, rode his manhood, enjoying every moment of her release to the very end.

"Evie," he gasped as he joined her. He groaned as warmth filled her core, leaving her sated and relaxed.

He lifted a little from her, meeting her eyes, and she wondered what he was thinking, what he debated to say to her.

Evie pushed back a lock of hair falling over his eye, throwing him a small smile. "Harvey, I must say what I need to, but before I do, I want you to know that I've fallen in love with you, and I never wish to be parted from you, not even the two short miles that Cardell Castle is from Aberdeen."

Harvey sat them both up, helping Evie right her gown, before laying the fur rug over her knees. He did not reply to her statement, unsure how he was going to explain he could not offer her anything, as impoverished as he was.

His only hope, as callous as it made him seem, was to

marry an heiress, and Miss Hall from Brighton was certainly not that.

He drank her in as she watched him, wishing that were not the case. He should not have been intimate with her, played her as he had. He ought to be horsewhipped for being such a cad, but nor could he stand the idea of leaving her, having her move to Aberdeen in her small leased cottage.

He shuddered at the thought.

"There are some things you need to know about me also, and it is time that I admitted my sins." He took a fortifying breath to say what he must, what he should have always said from the first moment of meeting her.

"What is it?" she asked, giving him her full attention.

Harvey swallowed the dread rising within him and knew it was now or never. "My family was once one of the most powerful in England and Scotland, but my father had a penchant for gambling, and not small amounts. I inherited several entailed estates that were penniless. For some time, I've been working to make them profitable again, but it will take some years."

She reached out and clasped his hand. He hated that she wished to comfort him at this time. Most women would run for the nearest wealthy gentleman instead of wasting their time with a duke without means, but not Evie. She was true, and it severed his soul in two that he could not give her what she wanted.

What he wanted.

"I have not regretted our time together. Please know that. I have enjoyed your company and have fallen under your honest charm, but I cannot marry you. I must marry an heiress to help secure the estates."

She pulled out of his hold and stared at him as if he had

lost his senses, which, in truth, he possibly could have. Was he really sending her away? Giving her marching orders?

What if she is carrying your child...

"You would not reconsider your choice even if your preferred wife did not care if, for several years, we had to economize?"

"It may be more than several, and I must beget an heir and secure his future. I can only do that with funds. Please understand, I do not tell you this to be cruel, but to be honest."

She shook her head, disappointment clouding her pretty blue eyes. "I believed you were better than that, Harvey. I thought you would prove wrong my concerns and marry me after all that we have done together, after all that I have come to feel for you." She paused, dabbing at her cheek. "But I see you do not feel the same."

Had he made her cry? Dear God, he wished he had not.

What do you expect, you fool? You've broken her heart.

"I suppose it is better I know now your intentions than wait until I find you also in the arms of another woman."

"Also?" he queried, just as the carriage rocked to a halt before his home. "What do you mean, also?"

"Nothing," she said, opening the carriage door and jumping down without waiting for a footman to help her and leaving him to watch as she fled into the great hall and away from his ruthlessness.

CHAPTER

EIGHTEEN

E vie heard the raised voices coming from the great
hall and quickened her steps into the castle. The
moment she entered the large room, a cold chill
ran down her spine at the sight of who stood before her.

Lord Bourbon.

How dare he show his face here in Scotland? As for that
matter, how had he known where she was?

Lord and Lady Lupton-Gage, having been seated before
the fire, stood, and Evie had the answer to her question. The
duke followed close on her heels, coming to stand behind
her, a protection of sorts, although he did not know why
she needed his shield, but the narrowed, considering glance
of Lord Bourbon told her it would not be long before Harvey
knew the truth.

"Evie, you're safe. We've been so worried," Lady
Lupton-Gage said, coming over to her and embracing her
warmly.

Evie hugged Reign in turn but could not understand her
anxiety. "I wrote to you and his lordship, explaining where I
was going and why. There was nothing to concern you

here," she said, wishing she had told Harvey the truth. What would he think of her when he discovered her lie was far worse than his truth? He would hate her for playing him the fool. For including him in her attempt to be free of Lord Bourbon.

"Would someone please explain why everyone has traveled to Scotland to seek out Miss Hall?" Harvey uttered, looking to each of them for clarification.

"Of course, I may explain that to you, Your Grace. Miss Hall, as you call her, is, in fact, Lady Bourbon...my wife." Lord Bourbon's mouth twisted into a smug line, and Evie wanted nothing more than to scratch the cheating fiend's eyes out.

How dare he even term her as his wife? She would never be so, not after his actions in London. She glared at Bourbon and reached for Harvey. He wrenched from her, staring as if she had grown a second head.

"Let me explain, Harvey. What he says is not true."

"But Evie, it is true. You are married by law and must return to England if you wish to end this nonsense with your reputation intact," Lord Bourbon said.

"I do not care a fig for my reputation, and not if it means I must remain married to you." Evie looked at Harvey, and nerves pooled in her stomach at the confusion and hurt she read in his eyes. "I did marry him," she admitted. "But it was a mistake that became too clear when I found Lord Bourbon rutting with Lady Compton in Lord Lupton-Gage's library but two hours after our vows. I knew then that I had married a man I did not know at all, nor did I wish to. I fled that night from London, traveled north as fast as I could, determined to annul the marriage when I was far from the earl."

"But you cannot, wife. I'm neither a fraud nor impotent,

so your sojourn to Scotland to whore yourself out to a duke was all for nothing."

Evie flinched at his words, and Harvey took a warning step toward Bourbon.

"No matter what has happened between us all, I will not have you speak ill of Miss Hall. Not in my presence, do you understand, Bourbon?"

Lord Bourbon glared but nodded his concurrence. "You will return to London with us, and we shall go on as if nothing untoward has occurred. You will perform your wifely duties, give me an heir, and all will be as it should be."

"I will not," Evie retorted. "I will not go near you. How dare you think that I will be your wife. I neither want any children from you nor to catch any dire disease you would expose me to. You promised to be faithful and broke that promise on our wedding day. I will not forgive you."

"Were you in love with him?" Harvey's tone was of disbelief and hurt.

"No, I know now what I felt for Lord Bourbon was not love. It was friendship, yes, an emotion that I muddled with love, but it is not what I...not what I know I now feel for you."

"You ought to be grateful for having a titled gentleman marry you at all." Lord Bourbon laughed, pointing at her as if she were some court jester. "Tell me, Your Grace. Has our delightful countess told you of her past? She was a maid in a household in Brighton before coming to London. If it were not for the great fortune that landed in her lap, no one would have given her a second look unless they wanted her flat on her back as their whore."

"That is enough," Harvey bellowed, startling Evie from the shock of Bourbon's venomous words.

How could he say such a hurtful thing? She had not fled London without cause, and that reason was his infidelity. How could he treat her with so little respect?

"Your slander will not be tolerated," Harvey growled.

Bourbon threw back his head and laughed, staring at Evie as if to mock her even more than he had already. "Slander, Your Grace? No. What I say is true, is it not, darling wife? Will you not tell the duke the truth of your past and where you came from?"

"Do not speak about Miss Hall in such an unkind manner, Bourbon. I will not tolerate it," Lord Lupton-Gage warned in a voice that brooked no argument. "She is my wife's relative, and you ought to remember that."

"Miss Hall?" Harvey questioned her. "Explain what Lord Bourbon is insinuating."

Evie looked at Reign and back at Harvey. She had wanted to tell him everything, desperately so, for weeks now, but this was just the type of reaction and fear that stopped her. Would he forgive her past? Would he be appalled and send her away?

He should. A woman of her standing did not deserve to marry a duke. To love a man who was far above her in all ways.

"Lord Bourbon says the truth, Your Grace." She paused, taking a fortifying breath. "I was born in Brighton, and my parents worked for a gentleman farmer whose small estate overlooked the sea. When I was old enough, I was placed into service there as a lady's maid to his daughter before she married. Only by a lucky turn of events did I leave the seaside town and come to live in London with Lord and Lady Lupton-Gage."

"You were a maid? A servant?" Harvey stepped back

from her as if the term threatened his person with grime, and her heart broke anew.

"I was before I inherited a sizable sum from a relative I never met."

"The same amount that I inherited, Your Grace, along with another distant cousin of ours, who remains in London," Lady Lupton-Gage added.

"But Lord Lupton-Gage has been a marvel and helped me expand my wealth, and now I never need to marry if I do not wish to."

"Except you have already married," Lord Bourbon reminded her.

"Our marriage will be annulled, and in the marriage contracts, I remained in control of my inheritance. So it does not matter what I did, for it shall be overturned. We have not consummated the marriage," she countered.

"However, they do state you agreed to give me an allowance, which I intend to enforce."

That was true, much to her annoyance, but it would not come to pass, for she would do all she could to get out of this insufferable mistake she had made.

"I'm sorry, Evie, but nothing can be done to reverse the marriage. You must return to London and take up your duties as Lady Bourbon. As his lordship stated, he is neither a fraud nor impotent, which you require for an annulment to be granted. I'm so sorry, my dear."

Lord Lupton-Gage's words ripped her of breath, and she stumbled to a nearby chair. "I will not remain married to him. He has already proven to be untrustworthy and unfaithful. He does not care for anyone but himself."

"That is not true, my darling wife. You are very hand-some, and your money will go to any children we have. So, while I may not have your fortune directly, my family will eventually prosper under your generous funds."

"I loathe you," she seethed.

Lord Bourbon laughed, and Evie felt the prickling of tears. "Harvey, I'm sorry. I wanted to tell you so many times. I wanted to ask for your help and guidance. I never wished to hurt you. You know how much you mean to me."

"I must not mean very much to you if this is the truth of your character. I do not even know who you are," he said, his tone devoid of emotion. "How could you keep such a secret from me?"

"Do not be so harsh, Your Grace," Lord Bourbon stated. "Her lowly upbringing and coarse manners do not bring out the best in her. She cannot help that she has not had the education we have been fortunate enough to enjoy."

"You bastard," Evie seethed, wanting to be far away from Bourbon and everyone.

"You see," Lord Bourbon grinned, "there is that lowly upbringing I speak of. Maybe I should send you to the country until you learn manners and respect for people above your station."

Evie moved toward the stairs, knowing one thing for sure this evening, and that was her time with the duke was over. "I would prefer it, my lord. Anything to be away from you," she countered, leaving them to continue the discussion of her future, which was no future at all.

CHAPTER
NINETEEN

Harvey stared at everyone in his hall, unable to fathom what was happening. Evie was married? And Lord Bourbon was her husband! The thought made him want to cast up his accounts. She could not be his? The idea that a man who had always held women in little regard could have married Miss Hall made his blood run cold.

He fisted his hands at his sides, fighting to control the savage temper that wanted to pummel Lord Bourbon and his smirking, infuriating face to a pulp.

Not that it mattered what he did or said from this point onward. In the carriage only minutes before, in his grand gesture to do what was right, to be honest, he had told Evie that he could not marry her because she was not an heiress.

And yet she was, but a married one.

"Excuse me for a moment." Without waiting for a response from his impromptu guests, he made his way up the stairs toward Evie's room, needing to speak with her alone.

He found her in her room, packing her small valise. The

sight brought him up short with the knowledge she would leave. That she was going to return to London with Bourbon, and he could possibly never see her again.

"What the hell is going on?" he barked, unable to hide the panic in his tone. "You're married to Bourbon, and you're an heiress?"

Evie stared at him, her eyes as wide as he'd ever seen them, and his heart broke at the panic he read in her gaze. But what did she expect? Married? An heiress? Of everything he thought she might be hiding, and he'd been sure she had been hiding something, neither of those articles was what he'd been thinking.

She slumped onto the bed, the clothing she was packing held tight in her hands. "I thought myself in love with him," she explained. "He courted me, was kind and attentive, and eventually offered marriage, which I accepted. On the day of our wedding, I caught him in a compromising position with Lady Compton, and I fled London. I would not consummate a marriage with such a scoundrel."

Harvey ran a hand through his hair, unable to comprehend the truth. "It does not matter what you want or how you feel. You are married, and there are no grounds to force an annulment."

"But I have not given myself to him. I'm certain that is reason enough."

"No, it is not!" A pain thumped behind his eyes, and he massaged his temples. "Lord Lupton-Gage is stating the truth. Lord Bourbon is neither a fraud nor impotent. You will not get what you want." He swallowed the panic rising within him. "I have never slept with another man's wife before in my life and I do not appreciate that you fooled me as you did. What if you're pregnant? We were not always sensible."

"And what if I am?" she said, standing and throwing her clothes onto the bed. "How dare you," she seethed. "How dare that be your only concern. That I made love to you while married to another. A man whom I know less than you and do not love."

"I have every right to be put out, madam. You lied."

"And you lied too," she spat back, her eyes welling with tears. Harvey took a step toward her and stopped himself. No. He would not comfort her after all she had said and done.

"I will never forgive you if you're carrying my child, and my child will never know who their father truly is." Harvey did not know where his anger came from, but it was as savage as his desire to hurt Bourbon downstairs. "But there is nothing else for it. You'll return to England with Lord Bourbon and take up your position as his wife, and God willing, you will not quicken, nor shall we ever see each other again."

"God willing? Do you not care for me at all? Have these weeks meant nothing to you that you would pack me off into the carriage so quickly and send me away with Bourbon without a backward glance?"

Harvey closed his mouth with a snap and would not state what he wanted to proclaim. That he did care. That he cared far too much ever to be the same again when she left.

"It's because I was poor and not from money, is it not? That is why you're so quick to be rid of me. Not aid me to get out of a bad marriage."

"It is too late to help you," he bellowed, grimacing when she flinched. "You know I care, Evie," he said in a calmer tone. "More than you could possibly comprehend." The severing pain ripped him in two, knowing they could not be together. "I want you with a severity that will drive me mad with jealousy and pain, knowing you'll never be mine. That you're that pathetic excuse for a man's downstairs instead. I do not know how I shall bear it, but I cannot change what has passed before God."

E vie stared at Harvey, unmoving and without words. The lump in her throat burned, and she swallowed several times to regain some of her composure. Everything felt as though the entire world was crumbling about her, and no matter how much she tried to repair the loose bricks, they wiggled free and smashed.

"I have wanted to tell you the truth for so long," she admitted. "But how does one say such truth without losing everything you hold dear? I'm sorry I hurt you, but I do not think..." she closed her eyes, imagining a life with Lord Bourbon, and her stomach revolted at the thought, "I can live without you."

"I cannot live in sin with you, Evie. I require a wife, a marriage in truth before God so my children may inherit and continue the ducal line I'm battling to keep. You must return to London and stay away from me. Allow me to do what I must."

Marry...

Evie swiped at the tears that fell down her cheeks, biting her lip to stop it from wobbling. Despair cloaked her, and she hated herself for her poor choice in London. If only she had seen past Bourbon's dishonest charm and forced smiles.

"I will never see you again," she said, the thought unbearable. "I will never kiss or love you as I want." How could she leave him, return to London, and continue a marriage with Lord Bourbon as if none of the past weeks existed? She could not. No one was as strong as she was being expected to be.

"Go, Lady Bourbon," he said, his tone hard and brooking no argument.

Evie shook her head and turned back to her valise. She threw her dresses into the bag, not bothering to fold the articles. She quickly went about the room, collecting the few small things she had packed before starting toward the door.

"Goodbye, Your Grace," she said, meeting his eyes. "I wish you well in finding your heiress and suitable wife." Evie made her way downstairs and met Reign waiting at the foot of the stone stairs. "I am ready to return to London but will not travel with Lord Bourbon. Not under any circumstances."

"Now, just wait a moment," Lord Bourbon started.

"Very well," Lord Lupton-Gage interjected, cutting Lord Bourbon's protest off. "You may travel back to London with us, and we shall sort everything out when we're back."

"Thank you," she said, satisfied she could avoid her husband for a little while at least. Not that she could avoid him forever.

TWENTY

E vie entered her room at the Black Hog Inn at Huntingdon and locked her door. She could not endure a moment longer looking at a stranger, her husband, who smirked and talked as if nothing was awry with their union.

How dare he sit for hours and speak of their future, boast to Lord and Lady Lupton-Gage as if they were going to have a fulfilling marriage after the betrayal he had done.

The man was a fool. She would rather live in sin, live alone, and be ostracized by all society for the remainder of her life than have to spend one moment pretending to be happy, to be in love with a man who was as selfish as they came.

How had she not seen his flawed character before? How could she have been so blind?

A knock sounded on her door, and her stomach knotted. She did not want to see him, yet she instinctively knew that Lord Bourbon stood at her door, seeking entry.

"Evie, let me in. We need to discuss your conduct these past weeks."

She scoffed. The blaggard had no shame. "My conduct," she called out. "How about your conduct with Lady Compton on our wedding day? Do you not think we should be speaking on that matter instead?" Evie wrenched the door open and took in the man God and law called her husband. But he was no husband at all. Nothing but a tub of cheating horse manure if she were being polite.

"It was unfortunate that you witnessed my extramarital activities. Lady Compton is sorry you became aware of our arrangement, but know this. I shall never embarrass you again. I shall keep my mistresses secret from polite society. In fact, so well that you shall never know of them again."

Evie shut her mouth with a snap. Did he think being so honest about his conduct somehow made it better? That she would be happy with such an arrangement. "I do not accept your terms, and I will never live with you, Lord Bourbon. We made a mistake, and I shall either suffer the consequences of marrying wrong, or you will grant me an annulment without fuss."

"An annulment is impossible, so you will be ruined. But, I shall not let any wife of mine act so crass and without dignity. I shall give you until we reach London to come to your senses, and then you shall return to my town house for the remainder of the Season. If you do not, there will be consequences that you will not like."

"You're threatening me?" she asked, affronted. The urge to scratch the infuriating man's eyes out was paramount. How could she have married him? Standing before him now, listening to all his sage advice and plans, she realized she did not have one iota of affection for him. She couldn't care less what he did or said so long as he did it far, far away from her.

"You were the one who broke our vows, not I."

"And you have not broken them in Scotland?" Bourbon strode up to her, clasping her upper arms, shaking her a little. "Do not think to play me the fool, wife. I saw that you broke your vows the moment I witnessed Ruthven's reaction to my presence. How long did it take you to lie on your back? A few days? Did you do it out of spite?"

Evie wrenched free of Bourbon's hold, the image of her future with him as dark as the day grew outside. "I did love him, with everything in my soul, and I would do it again, live in sin, be his mistress if only I could have him forever. But he has more morals than you, and would never treat me with such little respect."

Bourbon glowered at her, and for a moment, Evie feared for her safety. Would he hurt her? Strike her? She took a step back, wanting to distance herself.

"If you do not behave to society's standards and my commands, I can lock you away for hysteria. Do not forget I can do so as your husband. So do play sweet, my little common whore. I married you because I believed you to be of sound mind and good character. I should so hate to have to punish you."

With his words, he turned about and left, slamming her door. Evie jumped and reached for a nearby chair for support. She slumped into it, despair swamping her.

Whatever would she do? How was she to get herself out of this predicament? She would not consummate the marriage; he would have to force her to do so.

Another knock echoed through the room, and the blood in her veins turned to ice. Was Bourbon back? Did he want to claim his husbandly rights tonight? Lady Lupton-Gage's sweet, caring voice followed the knock and soothed her anxieties.

"Evie, darling, may I come in?" she asked.

"Come, Reign," she called, thankful for any company that was not her awful husband.

The moment she saw Reign, the tears and the fear that she had been hiding from everyone broke free. She stood and ran into Reign's outstretched arms. Her cousin held her tight, rubbing her back in comfort.

The words, the fear, all that had happened in Scotland and during her journey to Aberdeen spilled from her mouth and would not stop until Reign was aware of everything.

The highwayman. Losing her maid and driver. Finding the duke and falling in love...

Even after their bitter parting, she could not deny her feelings for Harvey. They were as true and tangible as the ground she now stood, and no marriage to Lord Bourbon would change any of that.

Reign led her to the settees beside the fire, and they sat silently for a moment as she regained her composure.

"You know that we will not force you to live with Lord Bourbon in London, but we cannot stop him from pressing the matter and trying things that may be unconventional to return you home. He is most desperate to quell as much scandal as possible."

Evie swiped at her cheeks, well aware of his ruthlessness. "He has already threatened to have me locked away as hysterical. But I would prefer that to living with him. I made a mistake, Reign. Why must it be so hard for women to change an error of judgment?"

"I do not know nor do I have the answer you seek, my dear. But know Lord Bourbon will have to get past Lord Lupton-Gage and me before he takes you to an asylum. The cad, to be so unforgiving of your reaction to his infidelity is bold. I'm sorry we did not know his character before you said your vows."

Evie reached out and took Reign's hand. "It is not your fault or mine. Bourbon hid his demons well." She thought about his hands upon her person, the biting hold against her arms, and shivered. That was not a future she wished for. He was not to be trusted in any way. "I fear, however, that it'll only be a matter of time before I'm forced to go with him. How will I endure it?"

Reign stared at Evie, pity clouding her eyes. "Do not despair. We shall think of something. I shall have Lord Lupton-Gage consult his lawyers as soon as we return to London. I'm certain there is a way. We merely need to find it."

Evie hoped that might be true, and she held on to that tiny sprinkle of hope, for without it, there was nothing she could do but admit defeat.

TWENTY-ONE

Several weeks later, Scotland

H arvey sat at his desk and stared at the abundance of correspondence that needed his attention, his mind far from the work that was required to complete.

Would his mind ever clear of the vision of Evie, injured by his words? How could he have been so insensitive, telling her his prerequisite of a wife and his reasons as to why?

And all the while she was an heiress, the woman he needed to find and marry. How she must loathe him, detest that he had placed the stature of his pocketbook above that of her feelings.

Not that she was entirely innocent. She could have told him the truth of her fortune. Of her husband in London.

Married?

He shook his head, unable to comprehend such a truth. They had traveled alone for several days, ample time for conversation about one's past to be discussed. For truths and worries to be told. But nothing, never once did she hint that she was Lady Bourbon.

A letter from his steward at the Kent estate caught his attention, and he quickly perused it, his hope for remaining in Scotland for the winter falling away when his oversight at the southern estate was recommended.

Damn, he would have preferred to remain here. Away from society and one woman in particular who drew him even with the knowledge of her upbringing and current marital status.

"Your Grace, Lady Miller is here to see you," Malcolm, his butler, said from the door, pulling Harvey out of his troubling thoughts.

Harvey glanced behind the butler and saw Lady Miller standing there, expectant of being allowed entry. He stood, supposing if he were going to have a subpar day, it might as well be made worse by the visit of the woman who threw him over for a wealthier fiancé.

"Lady Miller," Harvey said, joining her before his desk. He bent over her hand in welcome before ushering her to a chair. "This is an unexpected surprise. What brings you to Cardell Castle?" he asked.

She sat and fidgeted with her gown before bestowing on him a smile that at one time would have made his breath catch. No longer, however. Now, it only reminded him how fickle she was and false of heart.

Similar to Lord Bourbon, he supposed, in many ways. The facade the earl used to make Evie believe herself in love was nothing but a thinly veiled falsehood that performed as well as anyone on stage.

"I was sitting at home and heard the news that Miss Hall returned to London and is quite the talk of the town."

Harvey fought not to react to her words at the mention of Evie, but nor could he help but hunger for news. Was she well? Did she miss him as much as he missed her? Had something untoward occurred in town?

The idea of her sharing a bed with Bourbon made his eye twitch, and he took a calming breath, knowing he did not need Lady Miller gossiping about him as well as Miss Hall.

"She returned to London some weeks ago. I'm surprised you did not hear that sooner."

"Well, I suppose I would have if you cared to attend any of the society events I host, but you do not. I received a letter today from a friend in London with all the latest *on dits*, and Miss Hall is, in fact, Lady Bourbon. Did you know?" she asked him.

Harvey saw no reason to lie and make the situation any worse than it already was. They had been married before God. There was no changing that fact. "Why are you here, Lady Miller? Is there a reason for seeking me out?" he asked, wanting to be rid of her so he could wallow in the knowledge that heiress or not, Miss Hall, or Lady Bourbon, Evie, was never going to be his.

Not unless Bourbon died...that at least would give him hope of winning her back.

"Well, the letter mentioned that Lady Bourbon refuses to move into her husband's London home. Apparently, she's determined to make a stance regarding his infidelity and refuses to give way to society and their expectations." Lady Miller threw him a considering look. "I suppose that would explain why she was with you. She seems quite the risk taker and a woman who's not afraid of doing what she pleases no matter the cost."

Relief poured through him, and Harvey let go of a

breath he had not realized he'd been holding. For weeks, he had endured nightmares of her giving herself to her husband, of being wrapped in his arms, forced to endure a man's touch that she did not want.

Or so she had proclaimed...

Harvey schooled his features and fought not to respond. "Lady Bourbon was accosted by highwaymen on her way to Scotland. I merely aided her after her coachman was shot and injured. I escorted her to Aberdeen, and within days of her arrival, Lord Bourbon and Lord and Lady Lupton-Gage escorted her home. That is all I know of the matter," he lied, seeing by the smirk on Lady Miller's lips that said she did not believe a word he uttered.

Not that it mattered. Nothing much counted anymore, and it would seem with this news from London that they had yet to find out about his involvement with Evie. At least she had been spared that embarrassment.

Until Lady Miller wrote back to her friend and divulged all she suspected of Lady Bourbon while in Scotland.

"Well, I shall write to my friend and find out whatever else is happening in London. I'm sorry now that I left before the Season was over. So much scandal." She paused, watching him keenly. "Well, I suppose I should be on my way. I have a maid, but it is not to do to be found at a bachelor's home, especially when we were once courting."

Harvey stood, grinding his teeth. They had been far from courting. They had been engaged. He studied his past betrothed and wondered whatever he had seen in the lady. There was a littleness about her, a spitefulness that he'd not noticed before, but now he did. He supposed it was always there. That she threw him over for his wealthy best friend ought to have been a telling sign.

"Good day to you, Lady Miller." He did not bother to

escort her to the door, and she hesitated, waiting for him to do so, but upon seeing he was not moving, she left.

He slumped into his chair at the sound of her moving through the great hall and out of his life. Good, he did not need her coming here and trying to wreak more havoc.

Harvey ran a hand over his jaw, thinking about what he had learned. Evie was the talk of London? The latest *on dit*? She would not like it, nor was it fair when she had not been the unfaithful one, not at first.

Perhaps he was a hypocrite for thinking it, but he could not blame her for wanting to remove herself from Bourbon. The man was a cad, and her friends ought to have warned her that a match with him was a mistake.

But unless he was willing to live in sin and have children who were unable to inherit his titles and estates, there was no future for him and Evie.

He rubbed his chest, the ache within always present. No matter how much he cared for her.

Loved her?

Blast it all to hell…was that the emotion he had been feeling? Love? And now she was suffering, alone and vulnerable in London. Perhaps he ought to travel through London to Kent to be sure she was well and safe. If only for his peace of mind. He may not be able to love her like a husband could, but he could care for her from afar and give her as much protection as he could while she endured a life she did not deserve.

TWENTY-TWO

London

Evie lounged in the private parlor in Lord and Lady
Lupton-Gage's home, watching London pass her
by from the comfortable window seat. Unlike
everyone else under the opulent roof, she was not getting
dressed for this evening's ball. In fact, Evie questioned if
London's upper ten thousand wanted her anywhere near
them.

A social pariah, she had become.

An utterly unfair slur, as it was not her fault her
husband could not remain faithful. Was she to be punished
forever for having a little nuance of self-respect?

London was burning with the scandalous events of her
marriage with Lord Bourbon and her refusal to move into
his Georgian mansion on Hanover Square, the most talked
about, if the gossip columns were to be believed.

The idea that she would ever live with the fiend was
nonsensical. That he had tried several times to force her
into doing what she wanted only made her resent him more.

Where was his sense of right and wrong over being intimate with Lady Compton?

Evie sighed, the gnawing ache within her ever-present. How she missed Harvey. What was he accomplishing right at this moment? Was he strolling the castle grounds, riding his magnificent horse, or working diligently at his desk trying to better the accounts?

A hackney cab pulled up before the town house, and Evie leaned forward, wondering who was to call. A gentleman alighted from the carriage, and she leaned against the glass pane, her eyes refusing to tell her mind what she was seeing.

Her father was in London?

He stepped onto the flagstone footpath and glanced up and down the street. He appeared to whistle in appreciation at the grand houses. She smiled, knowing he had never been one for pomp and ceremony, nor had she ever thought to see him again.

Evie started downstairs to meet him. She stepped onto the foyer floor just as her father entered the house. He took off his worn, battered hat and coat that had seen better days and handed it to a waiting footman.

"Father," she said, going to him and hugging him tight. "I did not know you were back. I did not think you would ever return from India."

"Ah, well, love, I heard of your fortunate turn of events and that you were in London having a Season. I was journeying back from India when I read of your debut in town. I came as soon as I could. I wanted to see my daughter. It has been too many years between visits, and I've not been a good father to you. I wanted to remedy that."

Her father glanced about the room, his eyes widening at

the grandeur. "A little different to what we're used to, hey, Evie girl?" he said, bumping her arm.

Still, she was unable to believe he was truly here. "Yes, very dissimilar. But you've come such a long way, and I fear you shall be disappointed." She paused, fighting to find the right words. "I made a mistake, you see. A terrible one I cannot change."

"Evie?" She turned and saw Lord and Lady Lupton-Gage standing near the downstairs parlor doors.

"Lord and Lady Lupton-Gage, may I introduce you to my father, Mr. Hall. Father, these have been my guardians, and Lady Lupton-Gage is a distant relative to us."

"A pleasure to meet you both," her father said, dipping into an awkward bow.

"Do join us, Mr. Hall. We were about to have tea in the parlor. You must be weary from your travels," Lady Lupton-Gage said.

"A cup of tea would be pleasing, thank you," her father replied.

They entered the parlor, and Lady Lupton-Gage rang for tea before they made themselves comfortable on the chaise longues.

"I'm sorry to ask this of you, Evie dear, but what do you mean I will be disappointed? Is everything well with you, my dear?" her father asked before Evie had time to settle into the lounge.

Evie darted a look at Lord and Lady Lupton-Gage and knew she could not fib. "Not at all well, Father. I did indeed have a Season, albeit a short one, and I am, in fact, married. To an earl, Lord Bourbon, but I do not live with his lordship. It's quite the scandal I've brought on myself."

"Not you, my dear," her ladyship said. "Lord Bourbon had a hand in this scandal more so than you."

Evie smiled at Reign, glad to have her unwavering support. "Thank you. That means more than you know." Evie paused, meeting her father's curious gaze. "I found Lord Bourbon being intimate with another woman on our wedding day in Lord Lupton-Gage's library. I fled London, determined to annul the marriage, but I could not. An annulment cannot occur due to the inability to consummate the marriage, which is what I hoped. There must be other factors taken into account."

"He was unfaithful on your wedding day?" her father sputtered, his cheeks growing pink. "Why I never. I ought to horsewhip the cad."

Evie reached out and patted her father's hand. "It is fortunate that what I thought was love was nothing of the kind, and I no longer care what Lord Bourbon does or who he does it with. I wish to live away from him for the remainder of our lives, but I fear I will not get what I want."

"Are you saying Lord Bourbon wishes to remain married and have you as his wife?" her father asked.

"Yes, he is adamant that Evie moves to his London home by this coming Monday. We're all apprehensive about the situation, knowing this is not what she wants. Anyone with an ounce of self-respect would not either," Reign added.

Lord Lupton-Gage held up his hand, bringing the conversation to a halt. "Evie, how old are you?" he asked.

She narrowed her eyes on his lordship, unsure how asking her age would help the situation. "I had a birthday in Scotland, and I'm now twenty, my lord."

"Apologies if this seems cutting," Lord Lupton-Gage continued. "But we did not know that you existed, Mr. Hall. Evie told us very little of her life in Brighton, and we assumed, wrongly now we see, that you had passed away."

His lordship met her gaze. "Has your mother passed?" he asked.

"Yes, several years ago," Evie answered. "And I am sorry I did not mention Father, but he was so far away, and mail can take several months to reach him. I did not think to write to him and ask him to return for a wedding, which I knew he would not make in the first place."

"Ah, well, I was already aboard a ship to England, which is why I'm here now. I decided to return one last time before traveling back to India. It is where I love most in the world, no matter how much I miss my sweet daughter."

Evie smiled, clasping her father's hand. "I miss you also, and you do not know how lovely it is to have you home."

"So you never knew of the marriage until you returned to England? Are my estimations correct?" his lordship asked. "You only knew she was having a Season?"

"Yes, that is correct, my lord," her father said, perplexed.

Evie studied Lord Lupton-Gage and noted the contemplation that entered his lordship's eyes. For the first time in weeks, hope ignited within her. "Tell me, my lord, my father not knowing of my marriage, does it make a difference to my plight?"

"You are under one and twenty, Miss Hall, and your father, who is alive and of sound mind, did not give his permission. With that, and that the marriage was not consummated, Lord Bourbon cannot enforce the marriage. With this new information, we can successfully annul the marriage and set you free of the cur."

Evie gaped, unable to comprehend the turn of events that could enable her to be free of Lord Bourbon. She could get an annulment? Do as she pleased? Be with the man she loved?

Harvey...

"Are you in earnest, Bellamy? That the answer to all our prayers was situated in India all this time?" her ladyship said, clapping her hands in delight.

The room spun, and Evie clasped the longue to steady her racing heart. "Father, your arrival here may have saved me." She threw herself at her father and hugged him tight.

"I am very pleased to have helped," her father said with a chuckle.

"I will send for my steward immediately and my solicitor straightaway. He will commence preparing the documents for the annulment, but I'm certain you shall be free of Lord Bourbon within a month or so and be able to move forward with your life as you wish."

Lord Lupton-Gage threw her a pointed look, and Evie understood what he insinuated. She would be free to love again, to marry whomever she wished. She could travel to Scotland...

She could finally be happy and have everything she ever wished. "I cannot believe this turn of events. I did not think I would ever be free of Lord Bourbon. Every night, my dreams were nightmares filled with images of having to live with his lordship and suffer through his infidelity."

"Well, that will no longer be something you must concern yourself with, my dear. I'm so happy for you," Reign said with a smile that matched her own.

"Good afternoon, everyone," Arabella said, flouncing into the room. "You all look pleased indeed. Is there news that would interest me?" she said, joining them.

"I'm to gain an annulment," Evie blurted.

Arabella raised her brow, glancing at everyone before she noticed Mr. Hall. "Oh, I do apologize. I do not think we've met," Arabella said.

"This is my father, Arabella. Mr. Hall, this is Arabella Hall, another distant relative of ours."

"Very pleased to meet you, Miss Hall," her father said.

Arabella smiled and leaned back in her chair. "Not as pleased as everyone else by the looks of all these smiles." She chuckled. "It seems you have arrived at the perfect time, Mr. Hall."

Her father chuckled, picking up his cup of tea and taking a sip. "And I'm very glad for it. To have thought my daughter was unhappy and that I may have saved her from misery brings me joy. Sometimes luck smiles upon those needing it, such as it has here today."

"It certainly has." Evie hugged her father again, unable to accept her good fortune and how bright the hereafter was. Lord Bourbon may threaten all he likes, but it would not pain her now. He could never crush her again.

TWENTY-THREE

Harvey arrived at the Lawrence's ball and kept to the edges of the room. He made general conversation with those who sought him out. Otherwise, his attention was wholly focused on Evie, who occupied his mind and every thought and had done so for the past several weeks.

She stood beside Lord Bourbon, who preened at the *ton*, eager to show off the wife he had brought to heel. Or at least that was what he had heard at Whites this afternoon.

Had she truly moved in with the fiend?

Indeed, he could not blame her if she had. There was little she could do as a woman. The annulment had been an impossibility, consummated or not. The excuse was not enough in the eyes of the law.

This evening, Evie wore a gown of green silk in the empire cut. The simple gold necklace and earbobs suited her austere nature, but even as others glittered as they danced or ambled past, she was the most handsome woman he had ever seen.

He sipped his brandy, tempted to go to her, to ask her to

dance, and be damned what Bourbon would say on the matter. He could throttle him well enough if he tried to stop him from doing so.

No, he could not make a scene and raise questions about his conduct around Evie. She had enough to negotiate with being married to the man. His intrusion would make her situation worse.

"Your Grace, what a surprise seeing you in London. We all thought you had ensconced yourself in Scotland for the remainder of the year."

Harvey turned and fought not to glower at Lady Compton, the very one who was Lord Bourbon's mistress. That she had singled him out above anyone else told him she knew of his ties with Evie. But what would she do with the information? That was yet to be seen.

"I have several estates in England and Scotland. There is no astonishment in seeing me in town. I'm merely traveling through to Kent." She raised her brow at him and smirked, and he fought not to give her a good set down.

"I thought you were here to visit Lady Bourbon. She is a favorite of yours, is she not?" she hedged.

Harvey met her eyes, read the cold calculation within them, and matched it. "As Lord Bourbon is a favorite of yours, or so I heard. Something about..." he tapped his chin, "a situation in a library involving a desk if my recollection is correct."

Her mouth gaped, and he was glad of it. He wanted her to know that he knew every little tidbit of her treatment of a fellow woman of her set.

"I cannot fathom why Lord Bourbon did not offer his hand to you instead of Miss Hall. I should imagine that Miss Hall's inheritance had something to do with it, even though the earl does not need funds. But then again," he continued. "What is enough when it comes to accounts? Am I right?" he asked, smiling.

Lady Compton's mouth pinched into a displeased line. "I do not know what you're suggesting, Your Grace, but it is highly vulgar."

"Well, if you were confused as to what I was suggesting, allow me to remind you that what I'm alluding to is you being caught on Lord Lupton-Gage's library desk, your skirts above your waist while Lord Bourbon, married but an hour or so before, serviced you. You ought to be ashamed of yourself for ruining the hopes of a woman who thought her marriage was a true love match. That illusion is now shattered, and I fear Lord and Lady Bourbon will suffer those consequences for a long time. Not that Lord Bourbon does not deserve anything less, but her ladyship certainly deserves more than was provided."

Lady Compton laughed as if he had said something highly amusing before smiling at those who glanced their way. "What does it matter if Lady Bourbon is wealthy or not? She is but a maid. A woman of no family or consequence. She may have more money than many of the *ton*, but those born with privilege and titles need to keep to our class. We may allow those who are not to enter, but they are never welcome. They are not enough."

Harvey downed the last of his whisky and handed the glass to Lady Compton. Her startled gasp made him laugh. "Privilege and titles do not make you a lady. It has, however, made you a whore to a lord. If you'll excuse me," he said, moving toward Evie and that dance he needed to have before he expired.

. . .

"Smile, my dear. We do not want the *ton* to talk of us and nothing else for the foreseeable future. They have had quite long enough already discussing our union."

Evie fought not to roll her eyes. Bourbon was a fool and a man who complained of the responses to his atrocious behavior. What did he expect the *ton* to do? She could certainly see the allure of knowing everything about the situation.

But soon, very soon, she would be free of him. Even now, her father and Lord Lupton-Gage had set into action her way out of this disastrous marriage. How fortunate her father had returned just in time. Had he stayed in India, she would have been forced to yield to the marriage and suffered in Bourbon's presence for eternity.

"Do not tell me to smile." Evie glowered. Deciding it wasn't worth her displeasure, she turned her attention to the many guests at this evening's ball. There were so many enjoying the festivities, dancing, and laughing. A surge of regret swamped her that she had been foolish and had rushed into a union that would leave her disappointed.

Evie's breath caught as Harvey strode purposefully toward her, a small, pleased smile on his lips. Hope and desire flared to life within her for the first time in weeks.

Harvey was here? Why? How?

His tall, muscular frame, strong jaw, and warm, caring eyes that she wanted to fall into every day made longing tear through her. She could not look away.

How she adored him.

Was he here for her? Had he come to London to try to protect her? She could only hope for both of those circumstances.

"Lord and Lady Bourbon," Harvey said, bowing. "Lady

Bourbon, I believe I reserved the next dance." He took her hand, his large, strong fingers entwining with hers and brooking no argument.

Lord Bourbon reached out, halting them. "I do not believe that is the case."

Harvey grabbed Bourbon's hand that held her arm and pushed it aside. "I believe you are mistaken," he said, his words low and final.

Evie went with Harvey, tightened her fingers in his, and wished never to let go. He pulled her into his arms just as the orchestra started to play a waltz. His gaze settled on hers, and the longing she read in his green eyes broke her already shattered heart.

"How is it that you're here?" she asked.

He watched her for a moment, as if he were drinking her in for the very first time. "My steward in Kent summoned me to the Ruthven estate, and I thought to stop in London on my way through." He paused, his hand on her back, dipping low and pulling her closer. "I needed to see you. I heard what you're suffering in London, and I did not want you to be alone."

"Does this mean you forgive me?" she asked, hoping he did. She did not know how she would endure another night, thinking he thought the worst of her and she would never see him again.

"There is nothing to forgive. You made a mistake, and our times do not make it easy for anyone to right a wrong, but I wanted you to know I'll always be there for you. Married or not. I want you in my life. I cannot live without you."

"But I'm married and cannot give you what you need, Harvey. It is unfair of me to expect you to give up on a wife and children. You must marry if I'm unable to solve my circumstances." She wanted to tell him, to announce that there may be hope for them, but until she was confident, she did not wish to even get her hopes up on the matter.

"I am incapable of doing that." He shrugged. "I will wait, even if that means I have to wait until we're old and have had a life apart. I will wait for you. I will wait my turn to love you as you deserve."

TWENTY-FOUR

L ater that evening, Harvey stood near the gaming room doors and beheld Lord Bourbon chastise Evie before the *ton*. Anyone watching the earl would soon recognize the signs of a man berating and belittling his wife, even if his words were no louder than a whisper.

Harvey clenched his fists at his sides, battling the urge to go to her, to remove Bourbon from her world for eternity. The bastard ought to be horse-whipped for being such a cad for ruining the hopes of his young bride.

Lord Lupton-Gage joined Evie and escorted her away, along with her ladyship. They started through the throng of guests, heading toward the entrance. Were they leaving?

Some part of him wished they were not, while another was thankful for it—anything to give Evie peace from Bourbon.

His gaze flicked back to his lordship, and Harvey found him watching him, the anger radiating from the earl toward his person sparking a fire within him that would not be sated. Not until his fist had made contact with the earl's pompous nose.

Surprisingly, Bourbon motioned for him to follow him before striding toward the terrace doors, his lordship's features resembling thunder. Harvey smirked, pleased the bastard was incensed and more than ready to confront him if he so wished.

"Ruthven, is there a reason you're here in England? I thought you were hiding away in Scotland with all the other impoverished nobility," Bourbon said as he joined him on the terrace, far away from the other guests taking the air.

A pounding sounded in Harvey's ears, and he fought to calm his ire. "I'm on my way to Kent, not that you're required to know." Harvey raised his brow, looking down upon the man who barely reached his nose. "Is there a reason you're worried I'm in attendance?"

The earl scoffed, but the flaring of his nose told Harvey he'd hit a nerve. Good. He wanted to strike many.

"If you think you're here for Lady Bourbon, I'm sorry to tell you that you'll be disappointed. She, unfortunately, said yes to me, and while it's regretful she found out about my vices sooner than I hoped, it cannot be changed. She will soon learn to live with her husband's choices."

"What if she does not want to?" Harvey asked. The idea of Evie in a loveless, wretched marriage made his stomach churn. She was a good person, a loving, caring woman. She deserved better than what Bourbon was meting out.

"She has. No. Choice." Bourbon accompanied his words with his finger poking into his chest. Harvey reached out and clasped his hand, twisting it until Bourbon squealed in pain.

"Do not touch me, and never chastise Evie before the *ton* as if she's nobody. She deserves your respect, especially considering she did nothing wrong."

"She bedded you. Can you deny it?" Bourbon wheezed through his pain.

Harvey pushed him away, enjoying the sight of the earl stumbling to gain his balance. He did not answer his lordship's question, not wanting him to know anything about his time with Evie or how much she meant to him. She was so much more than a passing tryst. A fact that took him far too long to notice.

"Keep your temper in check around Lady Bourbon, or it'll not only be your hand that's twisted, but I shall match it with your nose."

"You dare to threaten me?" Bourbon seethed.

"Aye, I dare," he said, his Scottish dialect deepening the more his temper was prickled. "I thought you knew this already, Englishman, that the Scottish are not known to keep their patience with the likes of your kind. Be careful before you find yourself in more trouble than you care to be."

Bourbon's face pinched in displeasure, and Harvey could see he wanted to seethe, say more to press his point. Instead, he took the intelligent option and pushed past him on his way back into the ballroom.

Harvey sighed and started around the side of the house and toward the front. Now that Evie had left, there was little point in remaining. If only they could have more time to talk. Would it be too late to call?

He ordered his carriage and decided it was not. The night was just starting, with many other entertainments yet to enjoy. It was not too late to try to see her again. He would not sleep until he knew she was safe and nestled in the Lupton-Gage household. Well, that was what Harvey told himself as an excuse in any case...

The house was deathly quiet as Evie lay in bed later that evening. She tossed and turned, the cool evening breeze billowing the curtains and helping to chill the room, and yet, nothing could make her rest.

She had seen Harvey, and how delightful and darling he was. He cared for her still, a fact she had thought no longer possible after their parting in Scotland.

If only Lord Lupton-Gage's solicitor would notify them of her annulment hope. His lordship had been so helpful, trying to keep the scandal from ruining her. But there was little to be done once the *ton* knew of her annulment. She and Lord Bourbon would be social pariahs.

Not that she cared one whit. As soon as she was free of Bourbon, she would return to Harvey, and they could leave for Scotland.

A tap on the frame of the open window caught her attention, and she sat up, looking through the curtains. Unable to see anything, she threw back the bedding and padded over to the window just as a pebble flew through the window and barely missed her head.

She leaned over the windowsill and felt her eyes widen as Harvey stooped over, searching for another small stone. "What are you doing here?" she whispered as loud as she dared, hoping she did not wake anyone in the household.

"I needed to see you. Come into the gardens," he said, disappearing into the shadows and out of sight.

Evie quickly pulled on her shawl, covering her delicate, white shift, and left her room. The house was silent, all the sconces and candles long extinguished. Evie moved quickly, making her way downstairs. Within minutes, she was running across the lawns where she had seen Harvey flee.

"Harvey," she whispered, not seeing him anywhere. "Where are you hiding?" she asked, absurdly amused by their situation. She should not be. She was a married woman meeting a man in the gardens who was not her husband.

"I'm right here." Solid and comforting arms came about her waist. Evie leaned into him, relishing his body against hers. She closed her eyes, savoring his embrace.

She turned and faced him, wrapping her arms around his neck. "You should not be. It's very scandalous of you."

"It is," he agreed. "But I could not stay away. I needed to see you. I want to let you know that I made a mistake in Scotland. I should not have let you leave."

"You had little choice but to let me go."

"Run away with me," he asked, his eyes warm and beseeching in the moonlit night. "We'll leave society behind, what is wrong and right, and be merry, just you and me. Forget what I said at the ball about waiting. I do not have the patience."

Evie clasped his jaw, wishing such a future would be so easy. "I cannot. Not because I do not wish to, but because I want to be lawfully free of Bourbon. I do not want to entangle you in my difficulties, even if you are so very willing."

"Oh, I'm willing to do anything to ensure you're mine."

Evie nodded. His eyes were as steady as his character. "There are things in progress that give me hope, but until they are finalized, you must keep away. It would be best if this dreadful affair did not tarnish you. If, God willing, we have children one day, I do not wish for their name to be attached to my scandal years from now."

"I hope what you say is true, and you can be free of Bourbon, but know that even if you are not, I want you to be mine. I want you to come away with me if nothing is settled. Promise me you'll at least consider my plan."

Evie swallowed the lump in her throat. She did not deserve such a good man. He was so far above her in all ways, and yet, he cared for her more than anyone ever had in her life.

"Of course, without question. I do not wish to live a wasted life. I want a life with you."

A small smile teased his lips. "I'm going to kiss you," he declared. "Most energetically, too."

Evie chuckled, but her laugh was swallowed by Harvey's mouth when he took her in a searing kiss that was indeed most enthusiastic.

CHAPTER
TWENTY-FIVE

Harvey lost himself in Evie's arms for the first time in weeks. Life pumped once more through his veins, making everything right in the world. She was all soft, womanly, familiar curves that he had missed more than he had understood himself. Her lips moved in a seductive dance that left him breathless, reeling for purchase.

"I want you. So much," he admitted, guiding her farther into the shadowed gardens.

"I want you too." Evie glanced about, ensuring their privacy, but his wish looked unlikely with nothing but lawn, hedging, and gardens about them.

"I shall have to be patient," he conceded.

She pushed against his chest. "Sit down on the lawn. We shall make it work," she ordered him.

The determination in her voice sparked his hunger. He did as she bade, settling himself on the damp ground, and watched, with amazement, as she straddled his legs and settled on his lap.

"I have missed you so much, Harvey. The thought of

enduring the remainder of my life and never feeling your touch again drove me to distraction. I could not bear it."

"I will not bear it. No matter if you're married or not." Harvey ripped at his falls, his cock springing into his hand, hard and ready.

Evie clasped his manhood, guiding him into her. Warmth and pressure encased his cock, and he groaned, shutting his eyes and relishing the feel of her in his arms.

So good. So wet and his.

Mine...

He would never share her. He knew this to be true to the very center of his being. He would never allow her to remain with anyone but himself, nor would he let anyone keep her from him.

"I love you," he admitted, cupping her face and meeting her startled gaze.

She stared at him, her mouth working for several heart-beats as she reconciled what he said. "I've shocked you." He chuckled, kissing her to try to bring forth a response. "But I do love you. I adore you, in fact."

"You have shocked me in the best way." Evie bit her lip, her eyes welling with tears. Happy ones, he hoped. "And I love you too."

Finally.

The words he had been longing to hear. "I will not live without you, Evie. I do not care what scandal ensues."

She moved against him, stealing his wits. He thrust into her, needing to claim, to take, to mark her as his. She gasped, held on to him, and rolled her hips as they tupped on the lawn.

She was so perfect, so beautiful and his.

"I cannot live without you either," she said, driving them both toward release.

His cock hardened further, his balls aching with desire. He thrust hard. Clutched her against him as they rode their way toward satisfaction. She was so tight, perfect in every way.

His...

"Harvey," she gasped, her movements feverish and fierce.

"Come for me, Evie. Take your pleasure with abandonment."

Her vibrant eyes burned with a sultry allure that would have brought him to his knees had he not already been sitting. She was so beautiful in the throes of passion. Unlike any woman he had ever known or would ever know again. For she was all he wanted, all he needed to make his life complete.

The first tremors of her release teased his cock, and he knew she was close. He clasped her waist, rocking her harder upon his cock, and then he felt it, the spasms that tightened and pulled his own release forward to join with hers.

Stars glistened before his eyes, and he came, careless as to where. It did not signify, for she was his and he was hers, and no one, not even marriage, would stop him from loving her as he did.

"Harvey," she gasped, her fingers spiking into his hair, pulling his short strands as she rode out her release.

He drank her in and savored the sight of her as she floated back to earth.

"When will I see you again? Tomorrow is already too far away."

He chuckled, kissing the underside of her ear, eliciting a shiver through her body. "Tomorrow, I will call. Mayhap we can be alone for a time too." He wiggled his brows. "For conversation only, of course."

"Oh, of course." She chuckled. "Until tomorrow, then?"

"Aye, tomorrow."

E vie woke with a start at the sound of rapid knocking on her door.

"Evie, may I come in?"

The sound of Reign pulled her out of her sleep and, with it, the realization she had locked her door last evening after returning from the gardens.

She threw back the bedding and opened the door. "Good morning, Reign. I hope you had a pleasant evening." Evie went to start her morning ablutions with a spring in her step. Her body felt like it was floating, and everything was right in the world. Well, as right as it could be being married to an ogre.

Reign's hand wrapped around her arm and pulled her to a stop. "Lord Lupton-Gage's lawyer and steward were just here, dearest, and the ecclesiastical court has granted you the annulment for incompetence. The bishop in Lord Bourbon's parish has tried the case and found you are within your rights, especially since your father was there to plead your side and state that he had not given consent."

Evie stared at Reign, unable to acknowledge that she was free. As of right this moment, she was no longer Lady Bourbon, but Miss Evie Hall once again.

No, it could not be true. She could not be so fortunate.

"Do you honestly mean what you say? They said it would take several weeks at least before an answer was forthcoming." She chewed her bottom lip, hating getting her hopes up only to have them dashed. "Are you certain?"

Reign laughed and flounced over to the bed before sitting, her features all but exuding merit. "Well, perhaps it ought to have taken longer, but the bishop's church was in need of new pews, and Lord Lupton-Gage thought it was best that we donate to the bishop's parish. It is only right and Christian of us, after all."

Evie squealed and threw herself against Reign, hugging her fiercely, toppling them onto the bed. "Thank you so much, my dearest friend. How will I ever thank you and Lord Lupton-Gage? You have done too much for me already."

Reign chuckled as they sat back up. "It is not your shortcoming that your ex-husband could not remain faithful and was bold enough to be so at his own wedding. Lord Bourbon deserves every ridicule he gets from the *ton*."

"Indeed he does." Evie thought back on the day and the painful emotions it carried. Bourbon was selfish and did not care whom he hurt so long as he gained what he wished.

"In any case, we believe your heart has healed, and any scandal shall be reserved for Lord Bourbon, not yourself. Not if you're to be a duchess."

Evie bit back the tears, knowing that she would soon be married, but this time to a good man. A man whom she loved far above anything she had ever had before.

How lucky she had been to come across him and gain his help.

His love. His dearest heart.

"His Grace will be calling on me today. Do you suppose I can see him alone in the parlor? I would so like to visit with him without anyone present. But only if you're accommo-dating, of course."

Reign tapped her chin in consideration. "That will be out of the question, my dear. However," she said before Evie had a chance to protest. "Where you disappear to when you visit with His Grace is perhaps not something we will be aware of at all times if you understand my meaning..."

"I do understand, and thank you for everything, Reign. Thank you for sponsoring me this Season and for helping me with Bourbon. I'm forever in your debt."

"You are not in my debt. We're family and friends, and what good are we if we do not help and love each other? It would be quite a frightful existence if everyone were selfish."

"You are correct, of course."

"Lady Bourbon," a maid called from the door's threshold.

Evie waved the maid into the room. "Can I help you with anything?" she asked.

"Yes, my ladyship. The Duke of Ruthven is here to see you. He's waiting in the downstairs parlor."

Evie jumped from the bed and raced to the armoire, realizing she still wore her night clothes. "Come help me dress. I'll go directly." She threw Reign a mischievous smile at the unspoken knowledge that she would soon be engaged.

To Harvey.

TWENTY-SIX

E vie tried to make her way patiently toward the parlor where Harvey waited, but the excitement, the expectation of seeing him again, was too much. Had she only seen him last night in the gardens? It seemed like forever ago. But soon, she could gift him with the news of her annulment and be free to be his wife.

Just as she stepped off the bottom stair in the foyer, the town house's front door burst open. Evie started at the intrusion before fear ran through her blood like ice water. The outrage etched on Lord Bourbon's visage gave her pause, and she stopped, unsure of her next move.

"How dare you," he seethed, slamming the door closed and striding up to her like a soldier at war. He pushed a footman to the ground who attempted to halt his threat. The poor servant's head collided with the bottom step, where, with a sickening crack, he lay motionless.

Evie moved toward the footman, but Lord Bourbon's strong, biting hands clasped her arms and lifted her all but off the ground, stopping her.

"How dare you annul our marriage? Tell me how you

were able to manage that. Did you bribe the bishop? I'll get to the bottom of it, and you'll be the one made the pariah of society, not I."

Evie tried to wrench free of his clasp but was unsuccessful. "I do not care about society or what it thinks of me. Now you're free to be with your mistress, and I shall not have to endure the embarrassment of it. I do not understand why you did not marry Lady Compton in the first place."

His mouth pinched into a thin, displeased smile. His eyes narrowed to slits of hate. "But do you not know, my dear? How naïve of you, but I suppose I should not fault you for your lack of education and insight for a woman who was once a maid. But I wanted only your money for our children, of course. Lady Compton, for all her lovely abilities, impeccable heritage, and rank, lacked that one asset I care about above all else."

"You make me ill. Let me go," she protested. "Someone help the footman," she called out when he groaned in agony.

He pushed her out of his hold, and she fell to the tiled floor, sliding a little way along before her back came up against something hard.

Evie looked up and noted Harvey watched Bourbon, his eyes filled with deadly intent. With patience she did not think he possessed right at this time, he stepped around her and walked toward the earl. Lord Bourbon, not always a fool, had the sense to step back toward the door.

"You dare touch Miss Hall," Harvey said, using her given name, not the horrible title she had acquired only weeks before.

Bourbon held up his hand, wagging his finger at Harvey. "It is not my fault she lost her footing. We were embracing, a goodbye, you understand. Do not do anything foolish, Ruthven."

Harvey chuckled, the sound laced with lethal intent. "Oh, I intend to do something, but it is not foolish."

"Best you do before I make amends for his actions," Lord Lupton-Gage said, coming out of the library and helping Evie to stand.

She thanked him and kept away from Harvey and Bourbon, who had started to circle each other like wild African animals. Evie looked to Lord Lupton-Gage and noted his unbothered countenance by the foreseeable altercation.

"You're a lying bastard, but I suppose that would not be so very foreign to you since it is what you do best."

"You dare call into question my morals?" Bourbon blustered.

Evie fought the urge to roll her eyes. Was he so blind to his own faults? "Come, Ruthven, he is not worth it," she suggested, wanting to be done with the earl forever. It would be too soon if she ever looked at the man again.

Bourbon glared at her, and it was the last emotion Evie noted on his face before Harvey's hand shot out, sending the earl floundering back to land on his behind.

His hands flew to cover his nose, blood dripping down the front of his crisp, white shirt and buckskin breeches. Bourbon's eyes flared with surprise that someone dared strike him, and yet, Evie could not bring forth one ounce of feeling toward the man, even when he was lying on the floor with a bloody nose.

That he had placed his hands on her twice in a matter of weeks told her what type of man he was and that he was no man at all—simply a bully.

"I ought to call you out," Bourbon said.

Harvey laughed, moving toward the front door and

opening it. "Get out, and note that you will get more than a bloody nose if I ever see you near Miss Hall again. Do you understand?"

Bourbon struggled to his feet and stumbled toward the door, not bothering to answer, merely fleeing the house like the coward he was.

Evie rushed to the footman who sat on the bottom stair, clasping his head in his hands. "Are you well? Is there anything we can do for you?" she asked. "I'm so sorry his lordship struck you."

He mumbled something about a tissane, and Evie waved over a maid. "Send for a doctor, and you must go and rest in your room," she suggested to the young man. "We will ensure you're taken care of. Thank you for trying to help," Evie said, praying the footman would be well after his altercation with the earl.

Harvey stood beside her, and she felt his hand slip into hers. "Are you well? I have never wished to harm anyone, but seeing Bourbon's hands on you made me want to commit murder."

Evie went into Harvey's arms, sighing in relief at his warm, strong embrace. The scent of sandalwood and leather, of the love of her life. "We are free of him now. That is why he was so angry. I was granted my annulment."

"You were?" Harvey held her away from him, staring at her as if she had gone mad. "But how? I did not think it was possible."

"I have a father who just happened to return to England after hearing I was engaged. Of course, he arrived too late to attend the marriage, but I'm under one and twenty, and without his consent, the marriage could be annulled." Evie paused, pulling Harvey toward the parlor. "After hearing how miserable I was and what Bourbon had done, he and

Lord Lupton-Gage helped me petition to grant my freedom. I was only notified this morning that I'm free."

"Hence why he was so furious." Harvey shut the door to the parlor, and he pulled her into his arms no sooner had they entered the room. "And why I'm so thrilled. This is the best news."

Evie could not quite believe this was her reality. "I'm unrestrained and can do whatever I want." Harvey kneeled before her, and her heart stopped.

His large, green eyes caught hers, and she knew nothing would ever be the same. "I'm in love with you, Miss Hall. Possibly since the moment you said you were perfectly capable of driving your carriage to Scotland alone. I never want to be parted from you from this day forward. Please, do me the honor and become my wife. I cannot live another moment without you in my arms, my life, my bed," he said with a teasing grin.

Tears slipped down her cheeks, and she wiped them away. She bit her lip, fighting the urge to turn into a blubbering mess. "Yes, of course I shall marry you." She joined him on the floor, clasping Harvey's jaw and holding his very dear face near hers. "I love you so much."

"I'm sorry about everything," he said. "I should have sent Bourbon away in Scotland. I could see your distress and his flagrant arrogance toward his marriage. I should not have cared what was expected of me, you, or what society thought, so long as we were happy."

If only life could be so simple, but it was not. "It was better that I leave. I know that now. I should never have run away in the first place. I ought to have stayed in London and fought for my annulment instead of fleeing the city. And you were right. A duke needs to marry at some point, and he could not form a future with a woman already legally married. I could not expect you to be satisfied with such a life."

"I let you down, and I shall never forgive myself," he said, frowning.

Evie reached up and smoothed the lines between his brows. "No, you never let me down. You escorted me north and kept me safe. You loved me as a man ought to love a woman and showed me what I deserve. What everyone deserves."

"Some of what Bourbon says of me is true. You need to know this before we announce anything."

"What do you mean?" she asked.

The frown was back, and he paused before he said, " Before meeting you, I had been in London looking for an heiress after a duchess's coronet. I only left due to my need to be in Scotland urgently. When you offered to pay your way to Scotland, well, shamefully, I needed the money, and so I accepted."

"I have not paid you yet." Evie studied Harvey, wondering if he believed she would throw him over after discovering this truth. How silly men were sometimes. "But I knew you were impoverished after our dinner with Lord and Lady Roxborough. Lady Miller made a point of telling me. I assumed as a way to keep my interest at bay, and while I do think that is true, I do not think it was to keep my fortune safe but because she wanted you for herself."

He scoffed and met her eyes. "She threw me over after my father died and left me in debt. Lord Miller was my closest friend, wealthy, and a much better catch than a penniless duke."

"Oh, Harvey, I'm so sorry. You did not deserve such treatment."

He shook his head, watching her in something akin to awe. "How can you be so forgiving of an heiress hunter?"

Evie shrugged and fought not to grin. "I am an heiress, not through birth, but by chance. If you can forgive my humble beginnings, that your future duchess can make a bed and set a fire as well as any servant in any of your grand homes, then I can forgive you for being impoverished and looking for a wealthy bride." She paused, taking a moment to brush her lips against his. "No one is perfect, Harvey."

"I do not need to forgive you for being a maid. I do not care that you were, just so long as you're my duchess from this day forever more."

"I'm not marrying you because you're a duke," she said, wanting him to understand that above anything else. "I'm marrying you because I love you."

He wrenched her into his arms, holding her tight. "And I'm not marrying you because you're an heiress. I know in time and with proper management I could get the estates back in order with or without my bride's contribution."

"I know you could," she said. "You would not have come to London, knowing I was still married and asking me to run away with you if you only wanted me for my money."

"I love you, and I'm eager to make this legal. I can prepare a special license, and we could be married within three days if you like?"

Evie favored that idea more than any other. "Three days, and then I shall be your wife."

"And my duchess," he said, taking her in a kiss that promised forever.

EPILOGUE

Ruthven Estate, Kent

They were married in the opulent drawing room of Ruthven's estate three days later, with only close friends and family present. The day was perfect, had dawned with blue skies and only the slightest whisper of fluffy white clouds.

But even if it had been the coldest of days, nothing could take from the happiness that radiated throughout Evie now that she was married to Harvey.

Her husband...

He laughed and conversed with several gentlemen friends she had become well acquainted with through Lord and Lady Lupton-Gage during the Season.

She caught a glimpse of Arabella as she slipped through a door in the drawing room and away from the party. Before she could follow and see what she was about, Lady Lupton-Gage approached her, kissing her cheek for the millionth time in congratulations.

"Oh my dear, this day was so lovely. The duke is smitten, is he not?" Reign said, watching her husband and Harvey talk animatedly not far from them.

"He is no more smitten than I am. I cannot fathom the turn of events these past weeks. My life, which seemed doomed for failure, has triumphed. I'm beyond grateful to you and Lord Lupton-Gage and dearest Papa."

Evie spied her father, walking along a large table at the end of the room laden with an assortment of delicious fare for their guests. Her father, the poor soul, wasn't used to such abundance, but as odd as it was to have a full stomach and never want for anything, he too would soon be accustomed to it.

Reign smiled, turning her attention back to Evie. "Without your father, his lordship and myself could not have achieved success. You are fortunate, my dear, and we're so happy for you. What do you intend to do now that you're married? Will you return to London or Scotland? Or remain here in Kent?"

"Well, that is what I wanted to speak to you about. We thought of remaining in London for a while. The house and lands need Ruthven's attention, and we're much closer to the Kent estate should he need to come down here than if we were in Scotland. But we thought to remain in town to see out the Season and help with the scandal. I know all of London is talking about us, and it's better if we're there to quell those rumors."

"You do not need to explain to anyone, but I understand your concern. In fact, I would welcome your assistance. Poor Arabella has been acting most odd. Since you left for Scotland, she's not been eager to attend any balls and parties, and she often sneaks away to retiring rooms and such. I do not know what is wrong, and she will not tell me. Mayhap you can get her to explain what is troubling her."

"Of course," Evie said, eager to help however she could. The past weeks, she had been so caught up in her troubles that she had poorly neglected her friend and distant cousin. She would make amends and ensure Arabella had a successful Season before its end. "I will do whatever I can."

"Thank you, dearest."

Lady Lupton-Gage moved on to speak to other guests, and Evie's attention shifted to Harvey. Seeing her alone, he came toward her. As usual, her body warmed to his allure.

Would she always want him as much as she did right now? She could admit that her interest had been sparked upon seeing him for the very first time.

Until he chastised her for the absurd notion of driving her carriage all the way to Scotland alone.

Her lips twitched at the memory, and he bussed her cheeks before taking her hand. "You look like you're up to something, wife," he teased, pulling her toward the door she had seen Arabella disappear through earlier.

"And now you're up to something. Where are we going?" she asked.

He did not reply, merely grinned mischievously as they left the drawing room. He ushered her across a passage and into an empty room. Evie looked about, having yet to see this room, although it looked like a gentleman's den. "Does this room lead off from your library?" She walked about the space, running her hand along the dark-green leather longue before perusing several bookcases filled with hefty tomes. "A reading room, is it?"

"It is, and you're more than welcome to come and sit in here with me if you do not care to use your private parlor upstairs." His arms enfolded her from behind. His lips brushed the side of her neck, sending a shiver down her spine.

"What are you doing, Your Grace?"

"Seducing you." His tongue licked along the side of her ear, and heat pooled at her core. The man was maddening and had no idea how much he discombobulated her.

"We have guests, if you have forgotten. We cannot disappear."

He turned her to face him. "We can do whatever we like. We're married, and you're a duchess. There is nothing we cannot do."

For the first time in Evie's life, she felt content and safe. Harvey was the best person she had ever known, and she was so lucky to have met him.

"What do you have in mind?" she asked, leading him to the lounge.

They sat, and she placed her hand on his thigh, enjoying the feel of the silk breeches beneath her palms.

He adjusted his seat, and her attention moved to his falls and the growing bulge within. Without saying a word as to her thoughts, she caressed his thigh before brushing his manhood. "Never mind answering me. I can feel what you want."

"Really?" he asked, raising one brow. "Now that you're touching me, there are things that I would like that you cannot imagine."

Evie wondered at his words, which sparked her curiosity. "What do you mean?" She cupped his groin and leaned against him as seductively as she knew how. He sucked in a breath, his eyes contemplating her question.

Would he answer her?

"I'm not sure you're ready for what I'm now thinking." He pressed into her hand, and she caressed his manhood with more vigor.

"If you do not tell me what you're thinking, how will you ever know if I am ready for what you want?"

"Very well." He reached down and ripped his falls open, his cock sprang free into her hand, and she stroked it anew, watching with fascination as it grew darker in color, rigid and ready. "Close your mouth over my cock and suck me."

Evie met Harvey's gaze, astonished by his crude words. But more than that, she was dazed by her reaction to his command. Suck his manhood? Could she even do such a thing? Without waiting for instruction, she bent before him and placed the tip of his penis in her mouth.

Wanting to taste him, she licked the tip of his member. It was salty but not unpleasant. She closed her mouth over him and did as he suggested.

He groaned, his manhood jerking at her touch. Warmth spread between her legs at his delight. She lowered her mouth farther, taking him deeper, sucking him as best she could.

He was so large, lengthy, and thick that it was not the most effortless action.

"Damn, Evie, you're so beautiful. Suck me, darling wife."

She took him deeper. Used her tongue to tease his manhood. He undulated into her, pushing deeper into her mouth. She wanted him to fuck her this way. She wanted him to fuck her in any way he wished.

He groaned, his fingers spiking into her hair, holding, guiding her mouth, making her cunny weep.

"I want to come in your mouth," he said, his voice breathless and husky with desire.

She murmured her agreement, not wanting to stop. She needed to taste him, have him come undone in her arms. Evie took him deeper and suckled harder and felt the moment his manhood stiffened and shot seed into the back of her throat.

Evie drank his essence down, keeping him in her mouth until she was sure the very last of his pleasure had passed.

"Damn it, Evie, you're an amazing woman," he said, clasping her face and kissing her deeply. "Now it's my turn."

"Your turn?" But before she could press him for further clarification, he lay her back on the chaise. He fumbled with her skirts, pooling them at her waist before the first brush of his lips, the kiss of his breath teased her sensitive flesh.

"My turn to make you shatter using nothing but my mouth."

Evie bit her lip, allowed her legs to fall open, and for Harvey to do as he willed.

Undeniable need to please Evie consumed him. He kissed along her thigh, tasting her skin, nipping and kissing his way toward the juncture between her legs.

She squirmed and opened for him like a flower. His cock, stiffening again even after the shattering release only a moment ago, taunted and teased him to sink into her wet heat and satisfy the hunger growing within him.

Yet, he did not. Instead, he kissed her mons, sliced his tongue along her glistening opening, and reveled in her moans.

"You're divine," he murmured, suckling her anew, swirling his tongue, teasing the little engorged button that begged and wept for touch, for release.

He slipped a finger into her tight core, fucked her with his hand as he loved her with his mouth.

She mumbled, gasped a reply he could not make out,

but he understood. Her body, a beacon of enjoyment, showed him she relished all he did.

"Harvey," she gasped, her legs tightening about his head. He treasured kissing her quim, working her toward a release that would be as encompassing as his own.

She undulated, her fingers fisting his hair, holding him in place. Not that he was going anywhere. Not until she shattered into a million pieces of bliss. And even then, she would never have to leave his side again.

How had he become so blessed to have won her? To have her as his wife. He would never regret how they came to be, as scandalous as it was, for the rest of his life.

"Oh yes." She tensed beneath him, and he suckled harder, wanting to see her come undone.

She moaned his name, music to his ears as tremors shook her body. He kissed her deep and long, worked her enjoyment with his hand, and gave her the first release of many this night.

This life...

He settled beside her on the settee and pulled her into the crook of his arm. She slumped partly over him, meeting his gaze. Her lids were heavy with satisfied bliss, their breaths labored after their exertions.

"I cannot believe we're married. There was a time when I thought all hope was lost, and you along with it."

"I would have stolen you away, married or not, as you well know. We would have been together and society could go hang. I only want you and no one else."

She threw him a wistful smile, leaning up to brush her lips against his. "I love you so very dearly, Harvey. Thank you for being you and loving me as you do."

He kissed her, rolling her onto her back to come over

her. "It is no effort to love you as I do. Thank you for agreeing to be my wife and duchess."

She chuckled, slipping her arms around his neck. "What a story we shall have for our children. How Mama met Papa on the north road to Scotland. Or the more scandalous story when you stumbled into my room thinking it was your own?"

"Aye I did, did I not?" he agreed, remembering the day well and how shocked he'd been to see a woman riding alone and driving a carriage. "How their father saved their mother from certain trouble, perhaps even death."

"I was not that much of a damsel. I did have a flintlock."

He raised his brows and chuckled. "A warrior indeed prepared for battle."

She narrowed her eyes; her mouth turned into a mulish line. "Do not boast, Your Grace. You do not wish to displease me already," she warned.

"Oh, no, no, no, I do not," he said, running his hand along the inside of her leg. "Not today, at least. We have other days to quarrel and then come together again, but today, well, today is nothing but laughter and pleasure."

"I'm not sure I've had enough pleasure yet," she said, seizing his hand on her leg and shifting it toward her sex.

"Well then, let me remedy that posthaste." Which Harvey did, of course, with great relish and zeal. As one's husband should.

Don't Miss Tamara's Other Romance Series

Dalliance and Dukes

My Virtuous Duke

My Notorious Rogue

My Ruthless Beau

The Wayward Yorks

A Wager with a Duke

My Reformed Rogue

Wild, Wild, Duke

In the Duke of Time

Duke Around and Find Out

The Wayward Woodvilles

A Duke of a Time

On a Wild Duke Chase

Speak of the Duke

Every Duke has a Silver Lining

One Day my Duke Will Come

Surrender to the Duke

My Reckless Earl

Brazen Rogue

The Notorious Lord Sin

Wicked in My Bed

League of Unweddable Gentlemen

Tempt Me, Your Grace

Hellion at Heart

Dare to be Scandalous

To Be Wicked With You

Kiss Me, Duke

The Marquess is Mine

Kiss the Wallflower

A Midsummer Kiss

A Kiss at Mistletoe

A Kiss in Spring

To Fall For a Kiss

A Duke's Wild Kiss

To Kiss a Highland Rose

To Marry a Rogue

Only an Earl Will Do

Only a Duke Will Do

Only a Viscount Will Do

Only a Marquess Will Do

Only a Lady Will Do

Lords of London

To Bedevil a Duke

To Madden a Marquess

To Tempt an Earl

To Vex a Viscount

ABOUT THE AUTHOR

Tamara is an Australian author who grew up in an old mining town in country South Australia, where her love of history was founded. So much so, she made her darling husband travel to the UK for their honeymoon, where she dragged him from one historical monument and castle to another.

A mother of three, her two little gentlemen in the making, a future lady (she hopes) keep her busy in the real world, but whenever she gets a moment's peace she loves to write romance novels in an array of genres, including regency, medieval and time travel.